PUT YOUR BEST DUKE FORWARD

Dukes in Danger
Book 6

Emily E K Murdoch

Text by Emily E K Murdoch
Cover by Dar Albert

Dragonblade Publishing, Inc. is an imprint of Kathryn Le Veque Novels, Inc.
P.O. Box 23
Moreno Valley, CA 92556
ceo@dragonbladepublishing.com

Produced in the United States of America

First Edition September 2023
Trade Paperback Edition

The characters and events portrayed in this book are fictitious. Any similarity to real persons, living or dead, is purely coincidental and not intended by the author.

ARE YOU SIGNED UP FOR DRAGONBLADE'S BLOG?

You'll get the latest news and information on exclusive giveaways, exclusive excerpts, coming releases, sales, free books, cover reveals and more.

Check out our complete list of authors, too!

No spam, no junk. That's a promise!

Sign Up Here

www.dragonbladepublishing.com

Dearest Reader;

Thank you for your support of a small press. At Dragonblade Publishing, we strive to bring you the highest quality Historical Romance from some of the best authors in the business. Without your support, there is no 'us', so we sincerely hope you adore these stories and find some new favorite authors along the way.

Happy Reading!

CEO, Dragonblade Publishing

Additional Dragonblade books by Author Emily E K Murdoch

Dukes in Danger Series

Don't Judge a Duke by His Cover (Book 1)
Strike While the Duke is Hot (Book 2)
The Duke is Mightier than the Sword (Book 3)
A Duke in Time Saves Nine (Book 4)
Every Duke Has His Price (Book 5)
Put Your Best Duke Forward (Book 6)
Where There's a Duke, There's a Way (Book 7)

Twelve Days of Christmas

Twelve Drummers Drumming
Eleven Pipers Piping
Ten Lords a Leaping
Nine Ladies Dancing
Eight Maids a Milking
Seven Swans a Swimming
Six Geese a Laying
Five Gold Rings
Four Calling Birds
Three French Hens
Two Turtle Doves
A Partridge in a Pear Tree

The De Petras Saga

The Misplaced Husband (Book 1)
The Impoverished Dowry (Book 2)
The Contrary Debutante (Book 3)
The Determined Mistress (Book 4)
The Convenient Engagement (Book 5)

The Governess Bureau Series

A Governess of Great Talents (Book 1)
A Governess of Discretion (Book 2)
A Governess of Many Languages (Book 3)
A Governess of Prodigious Skill (Book 4)
A Governess of Unusual Experience (Book 5)
A Governess of Wise Years (Book 6)
A Governess of No Fear (Novella)

Never The Bride Series
Always the Bridesmaid (Book 1)
Always the Chaperone (Book 2)
Always the Courtesan (Book 3)
Always the Best Friend (Book 4)
Always the Wallflower (Book 5)
Always the Bluestocking (Book 6)
Always the Rival (Book 7)
Always the Matchmaker (Book 8)
Always the Widow (Book 9)
Always the Rebel (Book 10)
Always the Mistress (Book 11)
Always the Second Choice (Book 12)
Always the Mistletoe (Novella)
Always the Reverend (Novella)

The Lyon's Den Series
Always the Lyon Tamer

Pirates of Britannia Series
Always the High Seas

De Wolfe Pack: The Series
Whirlwind with a Wolfe

Chapter One

November 10, 1810

JOSEPH CHISHOLM, DUKE of Wincham, was not going to lose his temper. Probably.

"Blast it all to—"

He managed to halt himself just in time, but it wasn't easy. One's temper was always just on the surface when battling such a frustration as this.

A gentle cough behind him only made things worse.

"You wanted to say something?" Joseph snapped.

He didn't bother turning to see what his stablehand wished to say. That's what he told himself. The fact that, at this moment, it wasn't possible for him to turn around…that was beside the point.

"I was merely going to suggest," murmured Knowles in that quiet, calm voice which Joseph had learned to despair at over the last few months. "If you—"

"I don't need your suggestions," said Joseph harshly. His fingers tightened on his crutch, the wood biting into his palm. "Or your help!"

Though he could not see what the stablehand was doing, Joseph could well imagine the man had been reaching out to steady him. *And that,* he thought firmly, *is not going to happen.*

He was the Duke of Wincham. He had been born and raised around stables, around horses. There was nothing worth knowing about horses he didn't already know. This was supposed to be the place he felt most comfortable. Most at home.

Joseph shifted his foot, trying to get his balance and hoping to God he didn't fall. The last time he'd fallen before a servant, he'd sworn bloody murder and then had to suffer the disgrace of being carried—*carried!*—back into the house.

A bead of sweat dripped down the side of his temple as Joseph looked up at the tall stallion that had been brought out for him.

"Y'did ask for Maximus, didn't ye?" asked Knowles behind him.

Joseph's jaw tightened. He could hear the nerves in his servant's voice. When had he become such a terrible master? When had the Duke of Wincham become so difficult to serve?

Oh, you know full well when, muttered that dark, sarcastic voice at the back of his mind. The one which had grown in volume the last few months. *When you had your acci—*

"I did," Joseph said shortly.

It had seemed like a good idea at the time. He was tired of being cooped up inside, sitting with his leg…with what remained of his leg on a sofa. Tired of well-meaning villagers inquiring at the back door, tired of the vicar, Reverend McKee, turning up in his mourning suit as though someone had died…

No, he would feel much better out in the fresh air, Joseph had told himself. And what better way to feel himself again than to be out on his land, on his favorite stallion?

The trouble was he hadn't remembered Maximus being so…tall.

"I can fetch the mounting block," came the quiet voice of Knowles.

Joseph's jaw had already been clenched, but now there was a sore throbbing pulsing up his temple.

"Mounting block?" he said quietly, every syllable clipped.

The stablehand moved, circling Joseph and facing him as he patted the horse. "There's no shame in it, Y'Grace. Plenty of people need a mounting block to—"

"But not me!" said Joseph firmly, agony already building in his hip as he tried to keep himself steady. "Not me, no sir!"

Even as he said the words, he could hear how ridiculous they sounded.

Joseph sighed, head hanging as he tried not to show the soreness in his side. Not him. Not for years. He had known his way around the stables better than most. Certainly better than some of the stable lads, who came to be apprentices to Knowles.

But since the accident…

"Y'Grace, if I may be so bold, you've lost y'leg—"

"Only from the knee down," said Joseph hotly.

As though that made any difference.

Despite his better judgment, despite knowing he would hate what he saw, Joseph allowed his gaze to meander to his breeches. His right leg was as it always had been. Perhaps a little sore after putting up with so much additional weight, but it filled his riding breeches as it always had done. The muscles along his thighs were visible through the fabric, a testament to his efforts.

His left leg, on the other hand…

A wave of nausea rushed through Joseph's stomach. Though he knew precisely what he was going to see, though he had seen the same for months, though his doctor had said—that dratted Doctor Walsingham, what did he know?

Though his doctor had told him he would grow accustomed to the difference, he never had.

His breeches on his left were just as taught on the thigh, but were tied in a knot just below the knee. And they could do that because his lower leg had been…

Joseph swallowed. Even thinking it was difficult.

…*Amputated.*

"Whether y'lost the whole leg or just a bit of it, it's goin' to change a man," began Knowles.

But Joseph was not going to put up with that. He was the Duke of Wincham, and he deserved respect!

Once, he had earned it. Now all he could do was demand it.

"You will not speak to me that way!" he snapped.

His gaze had lifted, glaring at the older man still patting Maximus's neck. The stablehand did not look away, accepting the fiery gaze of Joseph with calm equanimity.

Joseph swallowed the bitter words which had risen in his chest. He was not about to degrade himself by entering into a shouting match with a servant. That was not befitting of his rank or of his character.

At least, who he had been.

"I can mount perfectly well, I thank you," Joseph said, against the evidence.

Before Knowles had the chance to say a word, Joseph had forced himself forward. The crutch had been made for him by one of the carpenters on his estate to the exact specifications Doctor Walsingham had prescribed.

Best doctor in the country, indeed! Joseph had sniffed at the preciseness the man had demanded, but he had to admit, it was perfectly formed to his height.

The damned thing had to go with him everywhere, worse luck.

The crutch kicked up straw as Joseph made his determined way toward his horse. Maximus stood calmly, recognizing his master even without both legs.

Joseph almost permitted himself a smile. The fleeting thought was pushed aside by the sheer panic spreading through his bones as he stood beside his stallion.

The beast really was huge. Almost sixteen hands.

He'd been proud of his horse's build when he'd first bought him from the breeder. Joseph had wanted a stallion that would stand out in the hunt, catch everyone's eye when he entered London, or Bath, or Brighton.

Not that he'd be going to those places anymore. No, best to

stay here, at Cedarworth Lacey. It was safe here.

Joseph raised his right hand and patted the beast's side. "Easy there, Maximus."

His voice had lowered as it always did when he was with horses. What was it about them that made them so…so calming? He had never understood it, even as a boy. As a man, he had thought little of it. The Duke of Wincham hadn't wanted a quiet life. And he hadn't got it. And now look at him.

"Y'Grace, the mounting—"

"When I want that ridiculous contraption, I shall ask for it!" snapped Joseph. "Christ alive, man, I haven't needed that since I was twelve!"

More than half a lifetime ago.

But it was the wrong decision. The wrong words, yes, but more importantly, the wrong tone.

The sudden explosion of sound and fury startled the huge stallion, who took a hasty step to the side away from the noise.

This would not have mattered if Joseph had not been partly using the horse as something to lean on. Not that he would ever have admitted it, naturally.

He didn't need to admit it. The fact was made perfectly clear as Joseph lurched horribly, his balance entirely shot. Knowing full well what was about to happen, hating it, knowing he could do nothing to stop it, Joseph's arms flailed pathetically in spirals, and then—

The fall to the stable floor wasn't so bad. Many inches of straw made for a comfortable landing, and Joseph was relieved to see he had not accidentally fallen on horse dung.

Of all places he could fall, he knew from experience, this was one of the better.

It still did not remove the sting of embarrassment. How could he ever look a man in the eye again, Joseph thought desperately, his hip aching from the sudden fall, if he couldn't even remain upright?

"Here, take m'hand, Y'Grace."

Joseph glared up at Knowles, but there was no malice or merriment in the servant's eyes. He blinked seriously at Joseph, hand outstretched.

Much as it irritated him to admit it, even tacitly, Joseph knew he could not stand up without help. It was something he had railed against when first learning to walk again, but there it was.

"Thank you," he said gruffly, taking the stablehand's palm in his.

Within a moment, he was upright. He was also sweating profusely and sorely embarrassed.

"Right as rain," Knowles said cheerfully.

Joseph shot him a look, but didn't say anything. The man had earned a favor thanks to his silent help back to his feet.

Ye gods, to think that this time last year—even this time six months ago!

But the doctor had told him not to think like that, hadn't he? Joseph shook his head. As though it were that easy. As though one could simply ignore one's life until this point. As though the very act of walking could be forgotten, a skill he had taken for granted.

He had refused to be put in a bath chair.

"But you really will find it much more comfortable," Doctor Walsingham had said with exhaustion on his last visit. "Truly, Your Grace, a bath chair—"

"A bath chair is for invalids, those who are unable to walk," Joseph had snapped, his fingers tightening around the damned crutch. "I have a crutch. I am perfectly capable of—"

"Are you?" the doctor had interrupted with an arched eyebrow. "Then why do you never walk about?"

Joseph had stared in wonder. How the devil had he known that?

His doctor's eyes had twinkled. "I spoke to your servants—no, don't look like that, it's all in the aid of assisting your healing. But if you never walk about, Your Grace, then there truly is no point in the crutch either. You need to exercise! What did you enjoy doing before you lost your leg?"

And that was what had brought him here, Joseph thought darkly. An injunction from his doctor. What was the world coming to?

"Should I perhaps prepare a different horse for ye, Y'Grace?"

Joseph's attention snapped back to the present. "I beg your pardon?"

For some reason, his stablehand looked concerned. Concerned? About him? Oh, that would be the death of him.

"I said, perhaps I should saddle up a different horse," said Knowles. "Put Maximums back like, and prepare...oh, I don't know. Julius, or Cleopatra—"

"The day I start riding a mare will be the day I lie down and die," muttered Joseph.

The very idea! He was no woman, no lightskirt pretending at horses. Women never knew their way around a horse at the best of times. And his stablehand thought he should degrade himself with such an attempt?

Why not bury him in the ground now?

"I just think you may find it easier to—"

"Back to the house with you!" Joseph said, pushed beyond endurance. "Go on, get!"

It was not the most dignified thing he had ever said. In fact, if Joseph had heard another duke or earl, or really any gentleman, speak to a servant like that he would have been outraged. *They may serve us,* he would have thought, *but they are people too. Men and women of honor, if we give them their due respect.*

But in this moment, heart pounding, blood boiling, every part of his body aching, embarrassment still stinging his heart...

He would have said anything to make the man go away.

"And that includes the rest of you," snarled Joseph, his bad temper pouring out now that the dam was burst. "All of you, into the servants' hall, now!"

There were only two stable lads in the stables at that moment, but neither had served on the Wincham estate long, so did not know his normally placid temper. With frightened faces and absolutely no hesitation, they scampered off in the direction of the servants' hall.

"And you," Joseph muttered, hardly able to meet the gaze of his stablehand.

Knowles did not look in such a rush. "I'll go, Y'Grace, as that's what you wish. But I wish you would consider taking a hand of someone afore long. You'll not regret it, of that I am sure."

Joseph swallowed. It was sage advice. The sort of advice he would have given to another, perhaps, if they had been in his situation.

But before he had lost his leg, could he have truly understood what it was to lose such a part of you? Could he have even guessed at the lack of equilibrium, how every part of one's life was irrevocably altered?

The stable door swung shut. He was alone.

Joseph let out a long, slow breath. He had not even realized he had been carrying it, worse luck. He could feel his lungs aching at the forced compression.

As he breathed in, he noticed all the scents that made up the stables. The musk of the horses, the dry airy smell of the straw. The dark heavy scent of the leather, the oils, the sharp red scent of the iron.

All combined to create something which had always calmed, always provided a place to think.

Joseph glanced at Maximus, still standing out of his pen, ears spooked at the sudden noise.

"What am I going to do, eh?" he murmured, reaching out a hand and waiting for the stallion to come to him. "What are we going to do with me?"

It took about a minute, but Joseph was patient. Patience was something he typically only had with horses. People were so difficult, so unpredictable. Horses? You knew where you stood with horses.

Slowly, nose puffing and eyes darting about as though ensuring there was a route out if he so chose, Maximus gently stepped over to him. The stallion pushed his nose into Joseph's hand.

Despite all the frustration, the anger coursing through his bones, Joseph smiled. "There we are."

If only it was that simple. He could charm horses—or at least, he had employed the best people to charm horses for him then retained the information about how to work with them. Horses were easy.

"Look at me, eh, Maximus?" Joseph said softly to the horse as it nickered. "I'm the Duke of Wincham. I should be in town this week, entering society again. Dancing with the ladies and impressing the gentlemen."

Maximus snorted and shook his head.

"Precisely," Joseph said ruefully. "Not going to do much dancing on this leg, am I?"

No, his dancing days were over. Which was a shame, because though he was fain to admit it in company, he rather liked dancing.

The wind blew angrily outside, rustling the hay in the hayloft above, making the shutters creak.

But now that would be far too difficult. Everything was difficult now. Striding along the corridors of Cedarworth Lacey, stomping up the stairs, easily mounting a horse…all the things Joseph had hardly noticed before his injury were not so much difficult as impossible.

"You wouldn't think it to look at me," Joseph said softly to the horse, which nuzzled into him. "But I was a spy for His Majesty. In France, of course."

Maximus looked at him with his great, large brown eyes. He had purchased the steed as a foal, hardly able to stand, as it happened. Not unlike his owner now.

"I had thought it a rather fun adventure to go abroad, serve my king and country for a little while, then come back and regale the Hunt with my exploits," said Joseph with a wry chuckle.

"Hark at me. I thought it would be easy."

When it had been anything but.

Oh, the spying had not been difficult. Even after the Revolution, being an English duke opened French doors that almost nothing else did. And he had enjoyed it. Conversing with interesting people, playing cards, sharing messages. Really, Joseph had not seen much difference between London Society and French spying.

Until the ambush…

Joseph pushed the memories aside. He was not going to dwell on that, he told himself firmly, as painful memories attempted to curl around his mind. He was living in the present, not dwelling on the future.

The wind blew loudly around the stable again, and this time it was so strong the stable door actually opened. Joseph did not turn around. It always did that in winter.

Taking Maximus's reins in his free hand, Joseph stepped forward awkwardly, leading the horse with him. The stallion obeyed without question, settled now, even if his master was not. Within a moment, they were standing in the stable yard.

Joseph looked up at the tall beast and gritted his teeth. If he was going to return to France and regain his position as one of England's most impressive spies, he was going to have to learn to do many things again. Like walk briskly. Like dance.

Like mount a damned horse.

Joseph set his jaw. *How difficult could it be, really?* Knowles had already tacked up the stallion, and the stirrup was right before him. Maximus would know to remain still; he was well trained, his preferred mount.

All he had to do was be determined enough. That was the ticket.

Joseph hesitated only for a moment. The wind blew, tugging at his hair.

Then he attempted to lift himself up off his crutch to place his right foot, the only foot he had remaining, into the stirrup.

It was a complete mistake, of course. Before he'd even lifted his foot six inches from the ground, his balance became over-tipped and Joseph could feel himself falling once again, that horrible dizziness swirling around his mind, his arms flailing, crutch falling to the ground, and there was nothing he could do. He was falling, falling—

The thud of his back on the cobbles of the stable yard shot a spurt of pain up his spine.

Joseph groaned. "Argh, Christ."

He lay there, breath momentarily knocked out of him. The sky spun out way above him, his crutch fallen a few inches away from his hand. Joseph stretched. He couldn't reach it.

Of course he couldn't.

Maximus gazed down, snuffling slightly at the strange antics of his master. Joseph tried to grin, tried to see the merriment in the situation, but it was impossible.

Here he was, Duke of Wincham, celebrated spy and servant of the king…lying in his own stable yard, unable to get up, entirely alone.

"I say, do you need any help?"

CHAPTER TWO

HATTIE GODWIN STARED at the man sprawled on the ground. It looked most uncomfortable.

Instincts drove her forward. As she clicked her tongue and gently tapped her ankles on her mare's side, Bramble took a few steps along the path to the house she had never ventured near before, and then halted.

Cedarworth Lacey was a manor, an imposing monstrosity of a building, she had always thought. Home of the Duke of Wincham, which was all she needed to know.

But Hattie couldn't just leave the man there.

She had wondered for a while precisely why the man had been standing for so long beside the horse. The stallion appeared tall, from what she could see from a hundred yards away or so, but not insurmountably tall. Anyone who knew their way around a horse would surely be able to mount him. Anyone who knew their way around a stable could find the mounting block. How hard could it be?

But as Hattie watched, the wind tugging her dark hair, she had seen something far stranger. The man did not appear willing to mount the horse.

Her curiosity got the better of her. Though she had always studiously avoided riding too close to the neighboring manor,

Hattie nudged Bramble forward again to gain a better look.

He was tall. Dark hair, well dressed. He was, for all intents and purposes, a gentleman.

So why was he struggling so much to—

Hattie's breath caught in her throat.

The curve of the path had changed the angle of her view, and in that instant, she could see precisely why the man was having so much difficulty.

He appeared to only have one leg.

No—no, that wasn't quite right. Hattie's heart thundered in her chest, conscious she was intruding on someone's privacy but unable to look away. The man had a leg, but it ended at the knee.

What on earth could have happened to him?

Pity rushed through Hattie's chest, though it prickled uncomfortably. The man probably would not wish to receive her pity, she thought wryly. Most men never did.

Well, well. A guest of the Duke of Wincham only had one full leg. Though Hattie had never met the duke, she had heard of his love of horses. It had been the one redeeming feature, in her opinion, of the man who dealt so strictly with his tenants and seemed to have no interest in conversing with his neighbors.

He had evidently invited a friend to his estate during a most trying time, Hattie could not help but think. Though she would probably not have encouraged the man to go riding.

He's going to fall, Hattie thought.

She was proven right within a heartbeat. Though the idea the man could somehow manage to mount such a tall beast without a mounting block was laughable, the gentleman evidently seemed determined to try it.

Hattie was not surprised when the man collapsed into a heap on the cobbles, though she did flinch. That must have hurt.

Gaze flickering, she was also unsurprised to see the man was alone. Well, this November weather was most inhospitable. She was certain it was going to rain soon. There was dampness in the air, a whip of the wind above her that spoke of a heavy downpour.

If there had been anyone else out and about, Hattie would have simply turned Bramble around and made for her own stables. She had no wish to become drenched, after all.

But the man was quite alone. The stable yard, as far as she could see, was empty, which was unusual.

Hattie sighed heavily, knowing what she was about to do and already loathing the contact with the unknown gentleman.

It was going to end badly, she knew it. But she couldn't just ride away and leave a man on the ground, evidently unable to right himself. It was something she simply couldn't conscience.

And so, hating the inevitable awkwardness that was to come, Hattie prompted her horse closer.

"I say, do you need any help?"

She had spoken as brightly as she could. Hattie certainly would not have wanted a stranger to speak with tones dripping with sympathy. She assumed the gentleman, whoever he was, would be of the same mind.

She was not, therefore, expecting such a vehement look as the gentleman pushed himself up on an elbow.

"How dare you!" the man snapped, glaring.

Hattie raised an eyebrow as she brought Bramble to a halt. Well, she had known it. Why were men so dull and predictable?

Here she was, only wishing to help, and somehow the entire escapade was her fault.

"How dare I?" Hattie said quietly. "All I have done is ride over to you. I wished to ascertain—"

"How dare you ride onto land that does not belong to you!" interrupted the man, still glaring.

Hattie's lips quirked into a smile. "Oh, I don't worry about that. The master is almost never at home, and when he is, he hardly bothers to talk to his neighbors. And so we don't bother much with him. Here, let me—"

"You speak ill of the Duke of Wincham!" said the man with a surprised expression. "How unusual."

Hattie took a deep breath and managed to stop herself from replying.

How unusual. Two words that were often utilized to describe her, and very rarely with any sort of charity or warmth.

Yes, she knew she was unusual. She knew most ladies of society did not prefer to spend the winter Season at home in the country. She knew most ladies did not know how to dismantle tackle, or calm a raging stallion, or tell which mare would be in season next.

"How unusual."

But she wasn't about to permit some puffed up gentleman from the town come here and lecture her about how unusual she was or not, Hattie decided fiercely, fingers gripping her reins.

This was her land. Almost. Really, there were only a few yards in it; her pastures came close to the Cedarworth Lacey house here, and she had a perfect right to be riding where she had been.

Once she crossed over that path, she thought distractedly, she had technically entered Wincham land…

But what did that matter? He was never here; she had spoken the truth. Besides, this gentleman needed assistance. What sort of person would she be to just leave him in the cold?

"I am an unusual woman," Hattie said dryly. "And you are an unusual gentleman."

The man's face flushed as he glanced at his absent leg.

Her cheeks matched his. "I didn't mean—"

"I don't care what you mean," the gentleman said gruffly. "I am accustomed to—"

"I merely meant—you're out here all alone, most gentlemen have servants and—"

"I said I don't care," snapped the man from the ground.

Hattie swallowed, shame rushing through her chest.

She had given no thought to the absence of his leg when she had spoken. But in a way, she did not blame the man for disbelieving her. It would be something he would be naturally conscious of, wouldn't he?

She certainly would be.

Hattie tried not to look at the gentleman, whose cheeks were scarlet, but it was difficult to drag her eyes away. He was dressed in a most impressive royal blue coat, one which was clearly made of the finest fabric and cut by the finest tailor.

Why, she did not think she had seen its equal in many months. Most of the locals around her home wore the coats their fathers had worn. There was usually another decade or two of wear in a well-made coat, so they made use of it. Fashion rarely got a look in.

But this man was all fashion and no substance, Hattie could not help but think. His breeches were fine, his boots highly polished. She doubted whether he had been outside for weeks. The rain over the last month had muddied every path, yet there were only a few spots of dirt on the man's heel. His hair was finely cut, he was well-shaven, and had a genteel look about him.

Hattie grinned. So what was a primped up gentleman doing in the stable yard of the Duke of Wincham of all places?

"The duke invited you here, I suppose, so that you could go riding?" Hattie said.

The man's eyes snapped back to hers. "What makes you say that?"

"Well, everyone knows the Duke of Wincham is never here, but that he has an impressive stable," Hattie said airily. It was common knowledge; there was nothing wrong in saying that. "I heard he has two stallions from the Kerrelian line."

Just for a moment, there was a flicker of something in the man's eyes she did not recognize. If it had been anyone else, she would have said the man was impressed. But that couldn't be true. He was glaring again, as though she had contravened some etiquette she was not aware of.

Not that that would be hard…

"You speak very freely of the Duke of Wincham," he said coldly.

But his poor manners could not defeat Hattie's spirits. She shrugged. "I speak as I find. You'll discover if you stay long with your friend that most people here about speak openly of their opinions. Even of the fine duke, who never bothers to visit his neighbors."

She couldn't help but grin at the last few words. She half expected the man to grin back.

But he did not. He merely sat there on the cold, damp ground, his crutch a few feet from him. Evidently out of reach.

"Here, let me—"

"You do not think the Duke of Wincham would be offended to hear you speak so?"

Hattie rolled her eyes. What was it with men and their honor? It must be protected, guarded, respected. If they were ever to lose it, they would be beside themselves, though they did little with it when they had it.

And if it wasn't their honor, it was the honor of their friends, of other men. Did they never grow tired of worrying about such petty things?

"I doubt the Duke of Wincham has ever heard of me," Hattie said truthfully. Her mare stepped to the left, then right, unhappy staying still for so long in one place. "I've grown up here merely five miles from the duke's estates, and I've never seen him. What does that tell you about the man?"

The gentleman considered for a moment. His blue eyes, Hattie realized suddenly, were just the color of the sky at midsummer.

"I suppose," he said slowly, "I would say the duke has responsibilities elsewhere—"

"Oh, responsibilities elsewhere, that's what everyone says," Hattie cut across with a laugh. "But what about his responsibilities here?"

The man blinked. "Here?"

Hattie forced herself not to roll her eyes again. Men really were the densest—

"He has tenants here, doesn't he?" she pointed out. "The village. The church. The school. All things packed with people he could help. He could at least show an interest."

Now she was veering close to speaking out of turn, Hattie knew, but she couldn't help it. It was lonely up at her home. There were few people she could talk to, even fewer who would listen.

It was pleasant to have a gossip about her closest neighbor. Who didn't enjoy it?

"I see," said the man coldly. "Well, I think you may be judging this duke of yours a little harshly."

Hattie snorted. "Duke of mine? Oh, he's no duke of mine, I can tell you."

The very idea!

Oh, Hattie knew her mother had once harbored…they couldn't even be called dreams, not really. Fancies. Idle thoughts that mothers apparently had about their daughters marrying princes and going off to be princesses.

And though there were plenty of princes, they rarely ventured out to this part of the world, Hattie had told her mother forcefully. And so her mother had tended her sights a tad closer to the duke who owned all that land to the west.

Hattie's mother had died last winter and her foolish ideas had died with her. Hattie was not about to be distracted by a popinjay of a duke with no idea what was good for him.

"Well, I thank you for your interesting opinions on the Duke of Wincham," said the man coldly. "And I will thank you to be on your way."

Hattie blinked. He couldn't honestly be dismissing her, could he?

It would be a strange thing to do at the best of times, most uncouth—but the man was stuck on the ground, unable to get up!

She cleared her throat. "Let me help you with—"

"I don't need your help!" the man snapped vehemently.

Hattie could feel her own temper rise in response to the man's utterly nonsensical anger. "I hate to point this out, sir, but you obviously do."

Their eyes met, and Hattie was astonished to find a steely determination the likes of which she had never seen before.

Her breath caught in her throat.

The man was entirely serious. If he had his way, she would turn around right now and disappear off back onto her land. He would rather sit in the freezing cold, drag himself over to his crutch, and struggle to stand than accept her help.

What was wrong with gentlemen? Why could they not see a helping hand was not a sign of weakness, but instead a sign of community?

Not that he was a part of the community, Hattie hastened to remind herself. He was a guest of the Duke of Wincham, passing through as they always were.

He'd be gone within a week, probably. And she would never see him again. Which was a shame, because the man was remarkably handsome.

Hattie swallowed. Not that she had noticed, of course. She was merely here to help.

"I tell you, I do not need your assistance," the man said coldly. "I am perfectly capable of—"

"Go on then," said Hattie bluntly. "Stand up."

She knew instantly that she had crossed a line.

Ladies did not speak so to gentlemen. They were not supposed to speak so to anyone, Hattie thought as the man's jaw dropped at her frankness.

The trouble was, it was her nature. Ever since a child, Hattie had always spoken her mind. She had described the world as she had seen it, with no caveats or softness, and it had made her just as many enemies as friends.

It was why her mother had never taken her to town.

"You think I am about to unleash you on some unsuspecting gentlemen?" her mother had said with a laugh only last autumn.

"Harriet Godwin, you are a menace in your own neighborhood! What do you think people who do not know you will say after one of your outbursts?"

Hattie swallowed as she looked down at the furious gentleman.

One of her outbursts. That was the trouble; they did not have to be long. Only a few words and she could cut to the core of a person without even trying.

It was a hazard of being around her, she knew. That was why she spent so little time with people. It was usually safer that way.

"You are a bold one, aren't you?" the gentleman said slowly.

Hattie flushed. "I speak as I find."

"So I see," said the man. "But do you not ever wonder whether you have the right to speak to me that way?"

The right? Harriet stared. What made him have better rights than she did? He had certainly spoken to her just as bluntly as she had spoken to him.

Even as she thought this, she knew she was being facetious. Gentlemen were always able to speak more openly than women. It was one of the rules of society she had hated the most when her parents had tried to explain them.

The idea that merely because of a chance of birth, this man—*this idiot*, Hattie thought darkly—could say whatever he liked to her! But she would have to stomach whatever he said back!

Oh, no. Not on her watch.

Drizzle was starting to fall gently from the sky. Hattie had known it was going to rain.

The gentleman glanced upward, evidently noticing the precipitation for the first time.

"I would not wish you to catch a chill," said Hattie in her iciest voice possible.

The man snorted. "I'm sure you wouldn't want to catch one. You should go home."

"Not without helping—"

"I said I don't need your help!" snarled the man.

It pushed Hattie beyond all endurance. She'd had it up to here with gentlemen who thought they could lecture her merely because she was a woman. It was exhausting, always having to tiptoe around the sensibilities of gentlemen who had no idea what they were doing.

And now she had to stand here and watch a man who only had one full leg lie on the ground, unable to get up alone, in the rain, merely because of his pride?

"Oh, hang your pride," Hattie said cheerfully, dismounting elegantly from Bramble. "I'm sick and tired of men utilizing their pride as a way of avoiding accepting that they may need a helping hand. Here."

She stuck out her hand.

For a moment, just a moment, she really thought he was going to accept it. After all, she had done almost all the hard work. She had dismounted and approached him. If he asked, Hattie could easily retrieve his crutch for him, which he could use to help himself up.

Really, she was doing him a favor. A gentleman—*a true gentleman*, Hattie could not help but think—would happily accept her assistance, thank her, and wish her well on her way back home.

But it appeared this man was not fit to be called a gentleman.

"Go away, blast you!" scowled the man, pushing away her hand as though she offered him a vial of poison. "Have I not been clear enough? I don't need your help, I don't need anyone's help—I'm fine as I am, and I don't need a woman of all people to offer charity!"

Hattie blinked.

There was a roaring in her ears, a furious medley of anger, pity, and frustration.

And then she withdrew her hand. "Fine."

With the single syllable spoken, Hattie turned on her heels and returned to Bramble, who was standing patiently for her owner. In a swift movement, Hattie mounted her steed, took the reins—now damp—in her hands, and turned the mare around.

"Good afternoon, I am sure," she muttered, glancing at the forlorn-looking man, whose hair was now dripping.

He might have said something else. Hattie could not tell. She had already dug her heels irritably into Bramble's sides.

The mare launched forward, moving quickly through a trot into a canter. Within a minute, Hattie was back on her land and on her way home.

Anger still coursed through her body, but it was tempered now she was leaving the man behind her with curiosity.

Who was that man? How had he lost part of his leg?

And what had made him so indignant about the thought of accepting a strange woman's help?

Chapter Three

November 15, 1810

IF JOSEPH HAD thought he could not be in a more mortifying situation than he had already endured, he was now discovering he was wrong.

"Ouch!"

"If you don't hold still, it's going to hurt more," said the unsympathetic Doctor Walsingham. "Now for goodness sake, stay still!"

Joseph glowered at the man.

At least, he would have done, if the doctor had been facing him. As it was, Joseph was lying face down on his bed getting his back seen to, so Doctor Walsingham was entirely unaware of his heated gaze.

Joseph tried to relax, tried to force down the anger at his own ineptitude, and tried to lie as still as possible.

This was unendurable. But he would just have to suffer it.

"How long will this take?" he asked bad-temperedly into his pillow.

He heard what could have been a laugh.

"Every time you ask that, add two minutes," came the jesting answer from his doctor.

Joseph balled his fists but said nothing, despite the great provocation.

There had been two instances in his life when he had believed it would be impossible to suffer through something more embarrassing.

The first time he had attempted to walk. His stump just below his left knee had barely healed, but Joseph had been determined to make his own way from his large four-poster bed to his dressing room.

He had been found what felt like hours later, blood pooled around his leg, pale and cold.

Only days ago, he had experienced a situation just as mortifying and just as painful, though arguably in a different way.

"Go away, blast you! Have I not been clear enough? I don't need your help, I don't need anyone's help—I'm fine as I am, and I don't need a woman of all people to offer charity!"

"Fine. Good afternoon, I'm sure."

He gritted his teeth. *That woman!* She was absolutely impossible—speaking of the Duke of Wincham like that, as though she didn't know full well that was to whom she was speaking!

"I've grown up here merely five miles from the duke's estates, and I've never seen him. What does that tell you about the man?"

Joseph tried to take a slow, calming breath, but all he succeeded in doing was taking an irritated one.

The woman was absolutely infuriating. If he'd had his wits about him, he would have sent her packing with a short and sharp retort that would have made her blush and reconsider all her dealings with gentlemen in the future. As it was…

Joseph sighed heavily.

"I said stay still!"

"I am staying—"

"And don't talk!" said Doctor Walsingham sternly.

It was on the tip of Joseph's tongue to say the man could get out, apply to his steward for his final bill, and never darken his doorway again…but he managed to resist.

Not only because he was one of the best, apparently. The Duke of Caelfall had suffered a leg injury in France, the grapevine had said. The moment Joseph had heard, he'd written a curt letter to the man, asking for his recommendation of a doctor. Caelfall had said no one was better than Walsingham. So, here Walsingham was.

Of course, that wasn't the only reason Joseph forced himself to hold his tongue.

No. It was because, to date, Walsingham was the only doctor who would still agree to come to Cedarworth Lacey.

"Almost done," said the doctor quietly.

Joseph calmed himself with the thought that very soon, the blasted man would be gone and he could be left alone in peace.

If only he hadn't attempted to go riding again that morning. He should have known the weather was ill-suited for it, rain pouring down as the heavens opened.

He hadn't even made it to the stables; that was the most shameful part. *No*, Joseph thought. He had slipped on the way to the stables, the cobblestones slick in the damp air. The fall hadn't been the worst part, of course. It rarely was.

"I cannot think how you managed to get so much gravel in this wound," muttered Doctor Walsingham, dropping another bit into a bowl. The clink echoed around Joseph's bedchamber.

Joseph tried not to sigh. Neither did he, but there it was. When he had finally managed to drag himself, cheeks burning at the indignity of the position, to the servants' hall door, he had rapped on it fiercely. His butler had emerged, seen the blood pooling through the back of his linen shirt, and sent for the doctor.

"Well, I think that is the last of it," Doctor Walsingham said smartly. "Now, in a minute, I'll have applied a little salve and you can put a fresh shirt on.

Joseph submitted to the stinging salve with what he hoped was good grace. After having a leg removed, nothing really hurt that much anyway.

It was with great relief, however, that he was permitted to turn over, sit up, and put on a shirt.

"Thank you," he said stiffly.

Doctor Walsingham raised an eyebrow but said nothing. He started packing away his implements into his doctor's bag.

"I am grateful," Joseph added, in case the man hadn't quite heard him.

"I am sure you are," said his doctor quietly. "May I ask what you were doing when you suffered such an accident?"

There couldn't be much harm in telling him. After all, it was no secret. "I was heading to the stables."

"Really? I was not aware you had sufficiently recovered enough to mount a horse," said Doctor Walsingham with a nod. "Excellent exercise, of course. In dry weather, I would almost venture to recommend it."

Joseph could not help but chuckle. "You know, I think that's the nicest thing you've ever said to me."

He had spoken too soon. Doctor Walsingham snapped his case shut and turned to him with a quizzical look. "Nicer than 'I think you will live'?"

Joseph swallowed, burning irritation flaring in an instant in his chest. The damned doctor did it to annoy him, he was sure!

But the memory of that moment, panting, lying on the servants' table downstairs after such agony, the haze of opium still in his veins and the taste of laudanum in his mouth…

Joseph cleared his throat, as though that could clear the memory. "Perhaps."

Doctor Walsingham's eye twinkled. "I would have thought you'd need to make adjustments with your riding now that you only have one foot."

There was something about the way the man spoke, Joseph thought darkly. So matter-of-fact. Perhaps it was his medical knowledge, his training that made it easy to be so abrupt.

If anyone else had spoken to him like that, it would not have gone easy for them.

"I suppose I will," Joseph said shortly. "When I ride again."

Well, there was no way to lie, was there? He could not pretend he had been riding; Doctor Walsingham evidently had no compunction in questioning his servants. It wouldn't take long for them to reveal their master had, in fact, not even managed to mount a horse, despite many attempts.

The twinkle in the doctor's eye was gone and he sat slowly on the end of Joseph's bed, much to his chagrin. He had thought the man was leaving.

"May I offer you some advice, Your Grace?"

Joseph glared, forcing his expression to soften as he took in the calm, unruffled expression of the doctor. "I suppose you might, if you want," he said begrudgingly. "Though I make no promises to take it."

Doctor Walsingham smiled briefly. "I would expect nothing less. I am aware of someone who trains horses and teaches people riding who may be someone who can advise on the adjustments that would suit. They could help you ride again, I believe, and quite swiftly. I have always received good reports of their improvements."

Joseph had opened his mouth instinctively to roll out the same platitude he had given to the few friends who had visited. Martock in particular had been very gracious, he and his wife. The new duchess had been kindness itself during their short visit, and it was during their stay that he had perfected the response.

"Why, thank you. I will look into that."

And then of course, he never would.

But as Joseph prepared his tongue to trot out the trite little phrase, he found himself hesitating. It would do no harm, he supposed, to get this fellow up to Cedarworth Lacey.

Someone who specialized in helping people to learn to ride. Well, he knew how to ride well enough, but Doctor Walsingham was right. He would have to make changes to his technique; a man could not ride the same with one foot as opposed to two.

Perhaps having someone who understood horses, really

understood them, would not be the end of the world. He may even have a few things in common with the blighter.

Joseph closed his mouth, swallowed, and then said quietly, "You think he would assist?"

"I've never known Godwin to turn down a challenge," Doctor Walsingham said quietly as he rose. "I will write, if it pleases you?"

He probably should have thought about it for more than five seconds, Joseph thought in hindsight. Inviting someone to his home, giving them power over his recovery? He had not even permitted Knowles to help him on a horse, or his housekeeper, Mrs. Alan, to cook him those "healing broths" she talked so much about.

But perhaps an outsider, someone who had not known him when whole, would be just the thing.

"Write," he said curtly as Doctor Walsingham walked to the door. "Arrange an appointment. I'd like to meet this Godwin before I commit to anything more."

The doctor bowed gracefully. "Of course. Good day, Your Grace."

And Joseph had to admit, the man was prompt. Just the next day, he received a short note from his doctor saying Godwin would call on the morrow at three o'clock to discuss any insight that could be provided.

Perhaps if the man had written "help" instead of insight, Joseph would have canceled the appointment. He didn't want help. He didn't need help.

"Let me help you with—"

"I don't need your help!"

Joseph's fingers tightened around Doctor Walsingham's note as he recalled what that insolent woman had said. *The nerve of her!*

But insight? Yes, he had called on horse trainers before for insight. When a mare wasn't falling with foal, when a stallion would refuse to be ridden near a certain field. If he couldn't understand, he would bring in someone else for the insight.

Besides, if he truly intended to return to France, Joseph knew something would have to change. Riding a horse would be absolutely vital. He couldn't go about spying from a carriage! The very idea!

And so it was with a certain amount of trepidation, but also a feeling of calm, that Joseph settled himself into the drawing room at just before three o'clock.

"Don't fuss so," he said irritably, flapping a hand at Mrs. Alan.

His housekeeper ignored him. "Can't think of the last time we had a visitor here—and only a day to prepare! The cakes are cooling, and—"

"Mrs. Alan, I am here to be advised by Mr. Godwin about riding, not to hear his opinion on the décor or feed him cake," said Joseph testily. "There! The bell."

It was indeed the bell. That was one of the nice things about Cedarworth Lacey—at least, something Joseph liked. No matter where you were in the house, you could always hear when the front door bell was rung.

Mrs. Alan threw down a cushion. "The bell! I'll make myself scarce then, but you let me know if I can—"

"I have the dratted silver bell," said Joseph sharply, pointing to the infernal thing.

Doctor Walsingham had brought it a month ago, much against his wishes. He had argued Joseph should get up regularly and ring the bell by the fireplace. Joseph had stated that he had no such intention, and that had been that.

Mrs. Alan rolled her eyes. "That silver bell! Didn't the doctor say—?"

"Thank you, Mrs. Alan." Joseph looked pointedly at the door.

With a sniff worthy of Lady Romeril herself, the great doyenne who ran polite society, his housekeeper stormed off and disappeared into the hallway.

Joseph allowed himself a small smile. There was almost nothing Mrs. Alan could do to make him divest of her services. She was a small entertainment all of her own.

There was murmuring in the hall. He supposed his butler was helping his guest remove his coat and hat. It did not account for the slightly longer conversation than he would have expected, but perhaps this Godwin fellow was asking about the stables, the horses—*or*, Joseph thought as his stomach lurched, *the master*.

Well, it was only natural that the man would be curious. He certainly would be, if he had been called to somewhere like Cedarworth Lacey. The Duke of Wincham had evidently gained a reputation as a recluse, if his awkward conversation with that young miss had been any indication.

And though he had attempted not to think of her since that day, Joseph lost himself for a moment in the memory of her bold eye, the dark hair that had flapped in the wind, the effortless way she had dismounted from her mare—

The door opened.

"Miss Godwin for you, Your Grace," his butler said smoothly.

Joseph stared. He blinked. Then he stared again, the image before him unchanging.

It was a trick of the light. It was because he had been thinking on the memory of that irritating woman. That was why his mind was playing tricks on him, making him think she was standing before him.

But as the butler bowed and left the room, Joseph could not see anything else but her. Standing there before him in—in riding breeches of all things!

Joseph's mouth fell open. "What the devil are you doing here?"

"I suppose I could ask you the same thing," shot back the woman. "Still leeching off your friend Wincham's good graces, I suppose?"

Joseph could hardly take it in. What was she doing here? How did the woman have the gall to stride in here, into Cedarworth Lacey—and in breeches, too! Who was in charge of this harlot?

"You appear to be lost, madam," he said coldly. "But my butler will see you out."

He had almost reached the silver bell when her words halted him.

"How strange, you appear to be lost, too," she said with a grin.

Joseph's jaw fell. "How dare you!"

"Just as swiftly as you dare," she shot back. "I am here to meet the Duke of Wincham, believe it or not! Turns out he's finally realized his neighbors are people actually worth speaking to."

There was a strange sort of smugness in her eyes Joseph could not stand.

How this misunderstanding had happened, he had absolutely no idea—but he was going to put a stop to it right now. He was not going to suffer the indignity of having to explain to a woman—*a woman in breeches!*—that she was unwelcome.

Even if the tight clothing did give her behind a dramatically delightful look.

Joseph swallowed. That thought had been a little surprising. It wasn't as though he was staring at—*God damnit!*

"You should probably make yourself scarce," said the woman, her grin undaunted. "I'm here to meet the Duke of Wincham, and you appear to be in his seat."

"Well, as I am the Duke of Wincham," he said testily, "I am delighted to inform you that you are the one in error."

It was immensely satisfying to see the woman's face fall. Yes, it was easy to be bold and brash with someone who was just a gentleman, Joseph thought. But when you realized he was a duke…

"Y-You're the…*you're* the Duke of Wincham?" the woman breathed, stepping back.

Joseph wished he could rise to his feet. His foot. He was tall, taller than her at any rate, and would have added to the impressive moment by towering above her. As it was…

"Yes, I am," Joseph said, leaning back and trying to look supremely comfortable in this whirlwind of confusion. "And I heard what you had to say about the Duke of Wincham with surprise the other day. I doubt you would have said as much if you had known—"

"I would have said a great deal more if I had known you were the Duke of Wincham," said the woman boldly, though her pink cheeks suggested otherwise. "Well, Your Grace. Here I am, as requested."

Joseph frowned. The woman was half out of her wits! He would have to send her back to wherever she came from in a carriage; she could not be trusted to make the journey alone.

"You were not requested, nor desired," he said bluntly.

Something stirred in his chest at the word "desired." *Oh, blast it all.*

The woman was frowning. "But I received a letter from a Doctor Walsingham."

Joseph's heart skipped a beat. "I beg your pardon?"

"Look here," she said, pulling a crumpled piece of paper from her breeches' pocket. "It said the Duke of Wincham wanted to see me at three o'clock today. It was most particular about the time—"

"I requested Godwin," Joseph said curtly.

The woman nodded. "Yes. That's me. I am Harriet Godwin."

And then Joseph smiled, realizing what had occurred. *Of course!* The letter had been intended for her father, but there had evidently been a mix-up. Well, she would certainly feel foolish when he explained it to her. Women were so swift to make these little errors.

"I believe Doctor Walsingham's note was intended for your father."

Miss Godwin most unaccountably frowned. She took a step closer. "I don't think so."

Joseph nodded slowly. "Yes, because—"

"Because my father is dead," she said succinctly.

That drew some of the wind from his sails, but Joseph was undeterred. There was a mistake here somewhere. All he had to do was find it.

"Your brother then—"

"Your Grace, I have no brother," Miss Godwin said quietly, and for some inexplicable reason, a slow smile was creeping over her face.

"A husband then," he snapped.

For a moment, there was a flicker of—was that fear?

"I am not married, sir," Miss Godwin said sharply. "But if you are looking for the horse trainer, she is standing here before you."

Color drained from Joseph's face as he attempted to take in what she was saying.

It was impossible. A horse trainer, a woman! A woman, moreover, who had already insulted him so profusely just days ago!

But as he racked his brains, Joseph came to realize that at no point in their conversation did Doctor Walsingham ever mention that the horse trainer in question had been a man. In fact, he had been quite circumspect about mentioning anything about him…

"I've never known Godwin to turn down a challenge."

Joseph's jaw clenched. *That blasted Walsingham!* He knew perfectly well he wouldn't accept a woman about the place, bossing him about, so he'd tricked him!

"Go away."

Miss Godwin blinked. "I beg your pardon?"

"I said go away," said Joseph sharply. He would have to suffer this indignity alone, and hope Coulter, his butler, would not mention it to the staff.

Dear God, what would they think of a woman in breeches turning up to see him?

"You cannot teach me anything, so I would not wish to waste your time," Joseph said curtly, stomach churning.

And that was the end of it.

At least, it should have been. Any true lady would have graciously accepted his decision, curtseyed—*in a gown,* Joseph thought menacingly—and disappeared off, grateful to have exchanged a few words from the Duke of Wincham.

But not Miss Harriet Godwin.

"I think you will find I can teach you a great deal," she said, her temper flaring. "Far more than most men and certainly more than you know!"

Joseph stared. "You cannot be serious!"

"Far more serious about learning to ride again than you!" Miss Godwin shot back. "I knew the moment I saw you that you were trying the wrong technique to mount that stallion! If you'd just asked—"

"But I didn't ask," snapped Joseph, riled beyond belief. *The nerve of the woman!* "And I would appreciate it if you would leave—"

"I can prove it to you," interrupted Miss Godwin, now standing mere feet from his chair. "Give me a month and I promise I can get you riding again. You just watch me!"

"Fine!" exploded Joseph, pushed beyond all endurance.

Silence fell in the drawing room. Joseph could hear his pulse thumping in his ears, hardly able to believe he had just said what he had.

"Fine!"

"You…you agree?" Miss Godwin said faintly.

Joseph's breathing was ragged. "You think you're up to the challenge? Fine! But be prepared to be disappointed, Miss Godwin, and put your best foot forward. You're now the newest horse trainer to the Duke of Wincham."

Chapter Four

November 23, 1810

HATTIE GROANED. "WHAT were you thinking?"

She knew precisely what she had been thinking. She had been thinking if she didn't stop that irritatingly smug smile on that man's face, she would scream.

That man. The Duke of Wincham!

Hattie closed her eyes just for a moment as she sat at her desk.

To think of the things she had said to him! The outrageous opinions she had shared about the seemingly absent Duke of Wincham!

"He has tenants here, doesn't he? The village. The church. The school. All things packed with people who he could help. He could at least show an interest."

She would have said that anyway, even if she had known the man sprawled on the stable yard ground had been the very man in question.

Probably. If she had, she probably would have couched them a little better.

But when he had spoken like that to her in that horribly impressive drawing room, that superior smile on his face, her blood rose high…

Hattie sighed as she opened her eyes and looked at the spread of messy paperwork before her. She had been goaded into it. The Duke of Wincham had made her feel inadequate, as so many of the men around her always tried to do, and she had been tricked somehow into promising the world.

"I can prove it to you. Give me a month and I promise I can get you riding again. You just watch me!"

"Another mistake, Hattie," she muttered under her breath as she tried frantically to find the last horse doctor's bill. "Just add it to the pile…"

Pile was the right word for it. Hattie had never been a particularly tidy woman. She'd inherited that from her mother, who had said it was the servants' role to clean, and her role to create the mess.

"They'll have nothing to do if I don't make a bit of a mess," Mrs. Godwin had often said. "It's a kindness, really."

Hattie had always laughed at that particular phrasing of her mother's, but she couldn't say she was completely wrong. Her mother had been untidy, and it had been their servants' constant role to try to keep Godwin Place in some sort of order.

After her mother had died, however, Hattie had discovered rather to her surprise she was perhaps just as much, if not more of a contributor to the mess than Mrs. Godwin.

With her father gone and most the servants let go because of rising costs…

"I know I put it here somewhere," Hattie muttered, lifting up a pile of papers that looked uncomfortably like unpaid grocers' bills. "Somewhere…"

It took another five minutes to find the blessed thing. In that time, Hattie had managed to run through her conversation with the disagreeable Duke of Wincham twice more.

"I think you will find I can teach you a great deal. Far more than most men and certainly more than you know!"

"You cannot be serious!"

"Humph!" she snorted, blowing hair from her eyes as she looked at the paper in her hand.

The very cheek of the man! As though he hadn't heard of her. As though he didn't know she had a reputation for…

Well, a reputation. Hattie smiled ruefully as she picked up a pencil and started making notes in her ledger.

A reputation for bills, at the moment.

"You are a fool, Hattie Godwin," she muttered to herself as she tried to concentrate on the shifting numbers before her. "But you are not an idiot."

She knew better than anyone that if she was going to have any chance of keeping this place, she would need additional income. The stud horses were doing well, and the mares were from good lines, but somehow, money just seemed to pour away like water at the moment.

And the bills poured in just as freely.

Hattie pushed her hair back for a second time, snorted like her favorite mare, and then pulled a ribbon toward her. In less than a minute, she had the entire mess of dark hair piled up in a bun and tied securely in place.

It may not be the most fashionable of styles, for all she knew, but it was the most practical way to keep the dratted stuff out of her eyes, particularly on a windy day.

She glanced at the window. And it was going to be a very windy day.

Hattie spent another hour or so working on the books. It was unpleasant reading. Knowing precisely how much one owed and to whom did not actually change the main problem, which was that she owed far too much money.

Too much money going out and not enough going in.

It was all very well for her father. He'd been born a gentleman. He had assumed the small parcel of land he tenanted out to one family would be sufficient to keep him in tobacco and brandy all his days.

And it had. He just hadn't accounted for…oh, Hattie didn't

know. Anyone else.

"There," she said firmly to herself, putting her pencil down.

Although the grim process was over, Hattie had to admit it had been important. She knew now precisely what fee she would need to ask the Duke of Wincham for, if she was going to keep this place aloft.

Fifteen pounds a month. Fifteen pounds, if she only worked for a month.

Hattie closed her eyes, just for a moment, before collecting herself. It was a heady sum. How had she managed to create such a deficit?

But numbers had never been her specialty. Even when her father had attempted to teach her how to keep the books, Hattie had been far more interested in getting outside in the fresh air, riding.

He'd warned her it was important. Now she could see why.

A clock in the hall chimed the hour and Hattie looked up in alarm. It couldn't already be eleven o'clock, could it?

A quick glance at her father's pocket watch that she kept on his old chain told her it could.

Bother! She had hoped to have a few things ready before His Worshipfulness arrived!

Ah well, Hattie consoled herself as she tried to push the bills in a small stack before leaving the study for the hall. There was no possibility the brute would actually be on time, would he? If there was ever a man to keep one waiting—

"I am waiting, Miss Godwin," came the crisp, dry tone of the Duke of Wincham. "Our lesson began a minute ago, by my watch."

Hattie glared. There, standing in her hallway—*as though he had been invited in!*—was the Duke of Wincham.

He looked…

Far too good to be allowed, Hattie had to admit. Even if it was in the privacy of her own mind.

The man was tall, his blue coat once again around his shoulders, and his fingers were tight around his crutch. How he had managed to get in here without ringing the bell—

"No one answered the door," said the Duke of Wincham, as though reading her mind. "I let myself in. I was sure you wouldn't mind."

Hattie's eyes flashed to the door, then back to him. "What you think I would and wouldn't mind is entirely incorrect."

What had possessed her to say that?

Hattie would have groaned if it would not give the man such satisfaction. He did something to her, something unmerited. Why was he able to get underneath her skin so?

She was here to do a job, that was all. And when that job had been paid for, she would feel infinitely better about permitting this idiot duke so much of her time.

"Walk," Hattie snapped.

The glower that appeared to be only a few seconds away from the Duke of Wincham's face reappeared. "I beg your pardon?"

"I need to see you walk," Hattie said slowly, as though the man was an imbecile.

He did not appear impressed. "And this is to be my first lesson?"

"And while we're on the subject, we have not yet discussed payment."

She spoke swiftly, knowing if she waited much longer to say it, she would not have the bravery. Hiding her true thoughts was not something many people could accuse her of, but there was something about speaking of money…

Perhaps it was because she was English, perhaps because she was a woman. Hattie did not know. But it was always an uncomfortable topic, particularly with creditors.

It appeared it was even worse with strangers.

"I do not worry about such things," the duke said dismissively. "Apply to my steward; he'll pay you what you're owed."

Hattie swallowed, but she could not merely leave it at that.

There had been no terms of agreement made, no fees confirmed. "And so I will ask him to pay the fif—"

"He'll pay the fifty pounds monthly whenever you send him a bill," snapped the duke. "Now, why do you want me to walk up and down like a simpering miss?"

Hattie opened her mouth then closed it again. Her heart was thumping wildly and unusually; she needed to take a moment to consider her next move.

Fifty pounds? Fifty pounds every month?

The man must have mistaken her, she thought wildly. It was the only explanation. No horse rider would even consider fifty pounds a month to be a fair wage to receive, even working with the most difficult horses. Or… Hattie tried not to grin. The most difficult riders.

But a distasteful thought flickered through her mind.

Perhaps…perhaps she was wrong. Perhaps she had been undercharging her clients—perhaps they had been letting her. Perhaps every other horse trainer in the county was charging what she considered to be an exorbitant amount. And that was why her stud farm—

"I haven't got all day, you know," said the Duke of Wincham firmly.

It was his anger which prompted her response, Hattie told herself later. "Why? Do you have a great many invitations to attend to?"

Sarcasm dripped from every word.

The man flinched, but to his credit, he did not look away. "It may surprise you to hear that I have better things to do than walk about," he snapped.

Hattie rolled her eyes. Men truly were the most stubborn creatures. Reverend McKee could say it was mules all he liked, but she knew the truth.

"And it may surprise you to hear that I have a purpose for asking everything I do of you," she said with a sickly sweet smile. "Now, I may be a woman, and therefore, in your eyes, utterly unfit to do—well, just about anything. But humor me. Your Grace."

For a moment, Hattie thought the duke was going to turn on his heels and disappear, taking his fifty pounds a month with him.

But though he was glaring profusely, and evidently did not care for obeying, the man turned to the left and walked stiffly to one wall.

"There," he said firmly.

"And back, to the other wall," Hattie said, all enmity forgotten.

This time, thank goodness, he did not ask for reasons. The duke merely turned on the spot and walked across the hall slowly to the other side.

Precisely how long he had taken, Hattie was not sure. She was focused instead on the movements of his back.

"Take your coat off and do it again," she said, her eyes not leaving his shoulder blades.

They did when she heard his scoff.

"Really, this is most—"

"If I had known you were not serious about investigating my abilities, I would not have challenged you," Hattie said lightly.

It was difficult to repress a smile. If there was something she knew how to do, it was cajole men into capitulating to do what she wanted. Even if they did not realize it.

In a bad temper, the Duke of Wincham removed his coat and allowed it to drop on the floor. "And now you want me to—"

"Walk back and forth across my hallway, yes," Hattie said, rolling her eyes. "If it's too difficult, please do say."

The man gritted his jaw, as she had suspected he might, and repeated his movement. The sound of the crutch echoed around the hall, and the duke was going red at the effort.

Hattie watched carefully. His rolling hips, the tilt of his shoulder blades, the way he—

"There!" she said triumphantly.

The Duke of Wincham halted swiftly and looked about him,

as though she was pointing at a bumblebee flying around him. "Where?"

"Here," Hattie said, striding forward and acting instinctively.

Which, perhaps, she should not have done.

The instant her hands touched his hips, heat rushed through her fingers. She felt a strange sense of swaying, the feeling the world had jolted just slightly in its spinning.

Hattie's breath caught in her throat as she slowly looked up at the Duke of Wincham. She was standing not inches from him with her hands on his hips.

On a duke's hips!

"What the devil—"

"Here, feel this," Hattie said, pushing past whatever the moment had been and focusing on what she had spotted. "Focus!"

"But what am I—"

"Your hips aren't straight, do you feel that?" Hattie tried to show him, twisting his hips this way and that then allowing them to find equilibrium. "Your hip is too high on this side; it's what's creating the pain here."

She touched the other hip knowledgably.

The duke, however, did not appear convinced. "And you know this because…?"

Hattie swallowed. It was going to sound strange, no matter how she said it. She should just come out with it. "Sometimes, when a mare struggles to foal—"

"You're comparing me to a horse? A mare?"

"I know things about gait, Your Grace," Hattie said stiffly, removing her hands from the man's hips and taking a step back. Somehow, that made it easier to speak. "I can't get you on a horse if you're already unbalanced on the ground. Now when you walk, pull this hip down. Yes, lower than you think; you'll have to fight your instincts, but I promise that will balance you. And lean more on your crutch."

"Lean more on it?" The Duke of Wincham's face was a picture of confusion. "I want to be done with the damned crutch. I don't want to depend more—"

"It's there to balance you, and without leaning on it, you're imbalanced," Hattie said flatly. "That's all there is to it."

For a moment, the frosty duke merely glared.

Hattie could well understand why. It was not the sort of thing a doctor would say, was it? Most horse trainers wouldn't even understand why she was bothering to start here. They would have marched the man out to the stables, forced him up a mounting block, and hoped for the best.

But that wasn't going to work here. She had to get the idiot composed on the ground, as she said, before she put him anywhere near a horse.

"Fine!" said the duke finally, throwing up his free hand. "But what a waste of time! Why, I could be…well I'll be blowed."

His voice softened as he marched forward in a pique. He did not remain in a pique for long.

Hattie watched, with some satisfaction, as the duke tilted his hip down back into alignment with the other. Immediately, his steps became more fluid, his pace quickening.

"It hurts less," the man said in wonder as he reached the wall and turned, retracing his steps. "And my shoulders, they—"

"They'll feel better too, yes," said Hattie, trying her best not to look too smug. Well, it had all been so obvious, at least to her. "The hips are the center of the body, you'll agree. If they are out of alignment, the havoc they can play with the rest of your—"

"And my ankle, it feels more loose, more sinuous," said the Duke of Wincham, looking in surprise at his remaining foot. "Dear God."

Hattie allowed herself a small smile.

Well, it was a small victory indeed, but one she needed. Impressing the Duke of Wincham had never been something she thought she would have to worry about, but if Godwin Place was to survive to another winter, she had to earn a little more money.

Fifteen pounds a month would have been a godsend. Fifty pounds a month…Hattie hardly knew what she was going to do with it all.

Oh, yes she did. She was going to pay off all the bills, for a start. Then she was going to get a horse doctor out here, give all her mares and stallions a check over before the winter settled in properly. Then she could—

"Miss Godwin, I will admit, I am surprised," the duke said, continuing to walk, seemingly unwilling to halt. "I had no idea there was such an imbalance within me."

Hattie shook her head. "Few people would. It still feels odd, doesn't it, pulling your hip down like that?"

"I still feel off-kilter, yes," he said quietly. "Yet I cannot deny…I feel better."

"And the pain?"

She would not have asked if it were not her job, she told herself. Warmth suffused through her chest as the Duke of Wincham looked up from his foot, absolutely beaming.

"Almost entirely gone," he said quietly. "Yes."

Hattie's chest puffed out with pride. There were few things she could do well; she would be the first to admit that. But she knew horses. The more she knew horses, the less she seemed to know about people—but gait? That was the same, all over.

"I am impressed, I admit it, and I do not admit to that often," the duke continued. "Perhaps you are not as bad as they say."

And just like that, all the pleasure in a job well done disappeared.

"What do you mean?" Hattie bristled. "Who says that?"

"Your competitors, of course," the Duke of Wincham said calmly, halting in his tracks and fixing her with a beady eye. "You do not think I would hire you without ascertaining from those who also train horses whether you were worth a damn?"

Heat was undoubtedly turning her cheeks pink, but there was nothing she could do. *Worth a damn indeed!*

"I would argue some of them aren't worth a damn," she said coldly. "But then, they are my competitors. They've always wanted my stud. I suppose they smeared me to see me fail, hoping I would sell—"

"Most of them were unflattering, yes," the Duke of Wincham cut across her. "But a few admitted, much against their better nature, that you knew what you were doing with horses."

Hattie tried to find joy in his words, but it was rather difficult. *Well!* Going to others to see whether she was a crook or not. *The very idea!*

"You do not appear convinced."

"I am not convinced, no," he admitted. "Though you have already worked a small miracle. Whether your skills stretch to getting me on a horse? That remains to be seen."

Hattie nodded. Well, she hardly trusted him after a few meetings. It would be foolish to expect that from him.

Even if the tall, handsome devil had just been essentially cured of pain in three parts of his body. Really, was it so difficult for men to accept that she knew what she was doing?

"Well, be off with you," she said shortly.

The duke's eyes flashed. "I came here to ride."

"You came here to improve your gait—your walking," Hattie corrected swiftly, wishing to goodness she had better control of her tongue. "I need you walking like that, properly, for at least a few days. That'll even out the correction."

She caught his gaze and almost smiled. If she wasn't mistaken, the Duke of Wincham was just as stubborn as she was.

"Your Grace," she said, with a false simper.

The man snorted. "I think you can call me Wincham. After this, I owe you something, Miss Godwin."

"And you can call me Hattie," she said swiftly with a shiver. "None of this 'Miss Godwin' nonsense, please. Everyone I work for calls me Hattie."

There was a teasing look in Wincham's eye. "Indeed. Just so long as you remember, Hattie, that you do work for me. And the next time I see you, I want to be on a horse, riding."

He strode out of her home without a second glance.

Hattie drew herself up. "Well!"

CHAPTER FIVE

November 24, 1810

JOSEPH SPENT TWO hours that morning not thinking about Hattie Godwin.

It took a great deal of effort. Really, he thought as he stomped across to the stables, he should be congratulated. It was impressive, not thinking about a woman who constantly walked about in breeches and who ordered him about as though she were a lady and he not a duke.

He knew it was impressive that he had not thought about her for two hours, because he had thought about her for the remaining four.

Which wasn't his fault, Joseph told himself sternly as he opened the door into the stable and breathed in the comforting scent of horses, hay, and leatherwork.

It was her fault, of course.

Ever since that moment when she had corrected his—and he laughed at the word—gait.

"You came here to improve your gait—your walking. I need you walking like that, properly, for at least a few days. That'll even out the correction."

Joseph shook his head ruefully as he helped Knowles prepare

the two horses for the day's work.

If any other woman had spoken to him like that, even someone like Lady Romeril, the paragon of society's virtue, he would have given them a piece of his mind, strongly and with no filter, before marching off and declaring he would never see them again.

Never seeing Hattie Godwin again was a threat he was certain, though why he would not admit it, he did not know.

"She'll be here shortly, I suppose," said Knowles quietly.

Joseph tensed. "What do you mean by that?"

It was foolish to be so on edge, he knew. His stablehand was looking at him curiously, as though he was acting strangely.

Like a spooked stallion, Joseph thought darkly. Like a wild horse needing to be tamed.

"I only meant—it was midday you ordered her to be here, wasn't it?" said the stablehand quietly.

Joseph tried to nod at Knowles. "Ah. Yes, of course. That's when I ordered her here."

The words tasted strange in his mouth. Perhaps if they were not a lie, he would feel better about them.

As it was, it had been Hattie who had ordered him to be ready at midday. Joseph's lips pulled into a dark smile as he led Maximus out of the stables and into the cool stable yard.

The very idea of a woman—of anyone!—ordering him about…

He would never have countenanced it before he went to France. Joseph had been raised to know precisely who he was, and that was the Duke of Wincham. He was not of a man to be ordered about; his ancestors had done the ordering. That was what his father had done, and his father before him, for generations all the way back to William the Conqueror.

That was, if the family tree on the landing near the Blue Bedchamber was to be believed. Joseph, privately, had his doubts.

But still—the point was—

"Ah, there you are," said a cheerful voice. "And right on time, too."

A smile spread across Joseph's cheeks before he could stop himself. He frowned quickly to balance out the expression, trying to remind himself forcibly that this was nothing but a riding lesson. That was all.

Just because it was the third they had shared, and he looked forward to each one with mounting excitement…

"Terrible weather, isn't it?" said Hattie with a grin from atop her mare.

She dismounted swiftly, Joseph envying the way she moved so smoothly without care.

He had been able to move like that once. Sometimes he would dream about marching about his estate, riding with his friends, enjoying the hunt—and it would only be part of the way through the dream itself that he would realize. He had two legs, two full legs, and two feet.

And he could weep, thinking the loss of his leg had been the dream, a nightmare which had finally come to an end, and—

"Wincham? Hello, can you hear me?"

Joseph started, his crutch slipping on the damp cobblestone as he suddenly realized Hattie was standing before him, waving a hand. Standing very close.

He breathed in, unable to help himself, and her overpowering scent of soap and straw conquered him. Joseph's hand slipped on the crutch and it fell.

But he did not.

Joseph blinked. How the devil had he—

"Ah, I see you've been practicing your gait," said Hattie conversationally, picking up the crutch and placing it in his hand without another word.

Joseph's cheeks burned. It was bad enough he had to be compared to a horse at the best of times, but the first two lessons had been on Hattie's land, in her stables. At least there he'd had the privilege of privacy.

He was never sure where her stablehands and lads were

during his two earlier lessons, but he had been grateful they had disappeared long enough for him to receive instruction.

But now they were on his turf, literally. And that meant—

"Go on then, Knowles, don't you have enough to do?" Joseph barked, cheeks burning as he twisted his head to glare at his men.

Knowles nodded before returning to the stables. The two lads scampered.

"I hope you are enjoying the fact that your crutch fell and you did not," remarked Hattie quietly when they stood alone in the stable yard.

Joseph swallowed. He had found the experience rather strange. For months, his crutch had become a part of him—unwanted at first, then undeniably essential.

If someone had told him three months ago he could remain upright without the crutch, he would have had him thrown out of the room. But here he was. Able to do it.

"How did I do it?" he asked awkwardly.

Hattie had stepped away to tie up her mare to a post and he felt the lack of her most excruciatingly. His whole body seemed to tense with every step she took from him.

She turned, and his jaw relaxed.

Not, Joseph told himself firmly, that he cared. No, it was just…polite. The wish to be in company.

Even if he had been a recluse for the last few months.

"How did you do what?" Hattie asked with a raised eyebrow.

Joseph swallowed. She was dressed, as she always seemed to be, in breeches. The first time he had seen her, the attire had felt outlandish, impossible to reconcile with the dark luscious curls and the rosebud mouth.

He'd never seen a lady in such a getup before. Most of the ladies of the *ton* would have fainted at the very idea of being so scandalous.

Now the breeches looked…well, normal. Expected. Joseph wasn't entirely sure what he would do with himself if he saw Hattie Godwin in a gown.

Well. That was not completely true.

"Wincham?"

Joseph's stomach twisted to hear her say his name, something he usually reserved for his friends. His *gentlemen* friends. Hearing such a name out of her mouth—

But if he did not say something soon, she would assume him to be a simpleton, and he had hardly managed to impress her otherwise.

"I didn't fall with my crutch," Joseph said awkwardly, voice low. "I mean, I usually do. When you find found me here—"

"It's your gait," said Hattie, and Joseph was thankful to be spared the additional remembrances of that embarrassing moment. "You've been practicing dropping your hip, haven't you?"

Joseph nodded. Mrs. Alan had complained he was going to wear a track in the carpet in the Long Gallery, but he had ignored her. Hattie's advice had helped. He could walk now almost without any pain.

It was nothing short of a miracle.

"Well, now that your gait is so much more improved, your balance is better, too," Hattie said with a smile. "Your body can do some of the work the crutch—"

"You said I had to lean on the crutch more," Joseph said fiercely.

He had not meant for his tone to be so accusing, but it was rather suspect. Was this woman merely making things up as she went along? Did she have any idea what she was doing? Perhaps this was a mistake. Perhaps Doctor Walsingham—

"I'm sorry, did you fall just now or not?" asked Hattie, her chin jutting up. Her hair was tied up in a bun, which Joseph was finding rather distracting—but nowhere near as distracting as her eyes. "I gave you advice and now you're without pain. That same advice means you no longer fall over like a two-legged milk stool. I believe you were about to thank me."

Joseph opened his mouth in astonishment.

Really, the woman came out with the most peculiar…

Not that he could deny the veracity of her words. Though he may not wish to own it, he could not fault her logic. She had, in merely three lessons, achieved more than he had thought possible.

"Fine," Joseph said gruffly.

Hattie frowned, a line appearing between her eyebrows. "No, that is not a thank you, Wincham. Come on, how hard can it be for a duke to thank a lady?"

His jaw clenched. *Very hard indeed, as it was turning out.* "Thank you."

She held her gaze with the same ferocity and Joseph found himself swaying.

Aha! He knew she hadn't really helped him; he was still just as unstable as ever!

Only then did he realize he was not swaying, but rather leaning. Toward her. Toward the woman who was so bold as to treat him like any other gentleman.

It was intoxicating.

And then Hattie turned away. "Good. Right, where's the mounting block?"

In a swift rush of pain, all the tension returned to Joseph's back. "I don't want—"

"Don't you argue with me about that mounting block. I told you at your second lesson, there's no shame in a mounting block!" Hattie called out over her shoulder. "It's all right, I'll find it!"

A nerve pulsed in Joseph's jaw. *The arrogance of the woman!* There she was, striding toward his stable as though it were her own! As though she could just march in there and take what she liked!

Well, she was going to find that more difficult than she thought, Joseph considered smugly as she disappeared into the building. He had been certain she would try to enforce the mounting block, so he and Knowles had prepared for that. She couldn't use the mounting block if she couldn't find it, could she?

No, he had been clever there. Joseph congratulated himself silently. Hattie Godwin would have to get up a lot earlier in the morning if she wanted to outsmart—

"What were you thinking putting the mounting block underneath the winter hay over here?" called Hattie merrily as she reemerged from the stables pulling the mounting block behind her. "What a strange place to put it."

Joseph's cheeks burned as he caught her eye and saw the mischief in them.

Oh, she knew. She knew perfectly well that he had tried to hide it. Blast her to—

"Nice try," Hattie said softly as she positioned the mounting block beside Maximus. "But I wasn't born yesterday, Wincham."

Joseph's jaw tightened. "I suppose not."

"What do you have against the mounting block anyway?"

She couldn't understand. No one could, Joseph thought bitterly. One moment you were the Duke of Wincham, London's darling, returning to one's estate once a quarter to ensure everything was ticking over. Then you were in France, drinking champagne with the French as you spied out their secrets. And the next…

"I'm a duke, a man, a rider," Joseph said, quite against his better judgment. "What sort of man would I be if I had to use a mounting block?"

Hattie said nothing but raised an eyebrow.

Somehow, this infuriated him more. "You don't have to use a mounting block!"

"I have two feet," Hattie said quietly, her gaze unwavering.

Joseph did not think; he merely acted on instinct. He took a step back, as though hearing her words was physically painful.

And in a way, it was. How dare she say that—point out his injury, make it obvious—

"There's no shame in not having two feet," Hattie continued, her voice still low as her gaze never left his. "The only shame is pretending life is the same as it was. You have a chance to relearn all this, Wincham. To return to the riding you love. Not everyone gets that chance. You're really going to pass it up for a little pride?"

Joseph swallowed.

She made it sound so easy. As though his entire personhood had not been blasted apart in France. As though he wasn't literally less of a man now. As though life could continue on like before, as though none of this had ever happened.

But he had to admit, even if he did not like it, Hattie had a point. She had a very specific way of making him feel foolish, this woman, and he did not particularly like it.

Losing his leg had been a terrible accident. Was he going to let it cloud his whole life?

Joseph managed to drag his eyes from Hattie and looked instead at the mounting block. Five small steps.

He sighed, hating the bitterness in his voice. "Fine."

"That seems to be a favorite word of yours," Hattie said with a teasing smile. "Here, I'll hold Maximus."

"Oh, Maximus won't need holding," said Joseph. "He'll stand."

It was a relief to find he was right. Maximus stood patiently as Joseph slowly managed to make his way up each of the five steps on the mounting block. When he reached the top, he could already feel the heat of exertion on the back of his neck.

Surely it hadn't ever been this hard?

"And mount."

"I know that!" Joseph snapped, panting.

Concentrating hard and letting go of the crutch without a second thought, Joseph swung his stub of a leg over Maximus and pulled himself onto the saddle.

There. He was on. Though what credit he could claim from it...

"Excellent."

Hattie was smiling, and it made a shiver rush up his spine.

Which surely could not mean anything. It was just exhilaration at being back on a horse again. That was all.

"Now dismount, and we'll start again," said Hattie briskly.

Joseph's gaze snapped over to her. "I want to ride—"

"I know," she said calmly, his crutch somehow in her hand. She must have caught it when he let it go. "And I said dismount."

When was the last time he had lost a battle of wills?

Joseph could hardly remember. He was a duke. Even at school, the other boys allowed him to take the best seat at the table, copy their answers in exams. At university, as long as he had been physically present, he had received good marks.

It was ridiculous that now, at almost thirty years of age, he was about to meet the first person he could not outstare, and it was…a woman?

Joseph blinked. "Fine."

"You're saying that a lot at the moment," said Hattie with a laugh.

He managed not to swear as he dismounted, wavering without his crutch.

"Here you go," Hattie said quietly.

Joseph jumped. She was somehow at his side, and her sudden presence was again enough to knock his equilibrium.

His fingers brushed against hers as he took the crutch, and Joseph wondered…

But no. No, that was ridiculous. What did he have to offer a woman now?

It wasn't just his leg, although that didn't help. No, Joseph knew no woman deserved a man filled with this much bitterness. A woman deserved compassion from their spouse, and Hattie…

Joseph swallowed. Hattie deserved more, somehow.

"Mounting block," she said quietly.

He blinked. "I beg your—oh. Right."

This time, Joseph had just reached the fourth step when Hattie put out a hand.

"Stop," she ordered. "Now mount."

Joseph looked up at Maximus, who suddenly felt very tall. "What, from here?"

Hattie arched an eyebrow as she took his crutch from him. "Hark at you, you didn't even want to use a mounting block ten minutes ago. Now you find it too difficult to mount from four steps up?"

Joseph gritted his teeth. "I didn't say—"

"Well, go on then," said Hattie with that indefatigable smile. "I'm waiting."

His heart was racing. For a moment, Joseph considered merely stepping down the mounting block and going back inside.

This was ridiculous! Did she really think that gradually making him mount from lower steps was going to make it possible for him to mount from the ground? Maximus was sixteen hands! There was no chance it would work!

Joseph's gaze darted to the house. He could put his feet—put his foot up in there and relax. He could read a book, perhaps…

Oh, who was he trying to fool? He'd be bored stiff within five minutes. He'd had far more excitement in the fifteen minutes Hattie had been here than the last month altogether.

Joseph took a deep breath then attempted to pull himself up onto Maximus. His footless leg couldn't quite get over.

"There, you see, I—"

"And again," said Hattie calmly.

Joseph glared down, fury pounding through his veins. "I can't—"

"No, you can't, not right now," said Hattie, her voice still calm and eyes shining with determination. "You think everything should be immediate? You think if you cannot have something the first time, it is not worth fighting for?"

A sense of impudence was curling in Joseph's stomach. "I-I…I didn't say that—"

"You're showing me that if you're not willing to practice," Hattie said firmly. "I've got all day, Wincham. Show me what you can do."

It was Joseph's desire to impress, eventually, that won out.

On the fifth attempt, sweat beading on his forehead, Joseph managed to mount Maximus from the fourth step.

"There you go!" Hattie crowed, grinning. "Right, dismount. You know the drill."

He did indeed. This time, Joseph halted at the third step and glanced over at Hattie with a raised eyebrow.

Hattie nodded. "Ready to practice?"

It took another twenty minutes or so, by Joseph's estimate, before he could mount his stallion from the third step.

"No shame in not being able to do it first time," Hattie said quietly as he sat atop his horse with pride. "The shame is in giving up."

"I was never usually one to give up," Joseph admitted quietly.

He hadn't been, had he—so where had this defeatist attitude come from?

Hattie met his eyes. There was something so serious there that Joseph almost started. "No, I didn't think so. I believe we are the same in that regard."

Joseph's breath caught in his chest. When she looked at him like that…why, he rather believed he could do anything. Throw away the mounting block, throw away the crutch, with Hattie's confidence, he could run a marathon.

"But I think that's enough for one day."

Joseph's face fell. "What? I've already come so far—"

"And that is why we are stopping," Hattie said firmly. "Your body can only take so much. Come on, dismount and we'll put Maximus away with a carrot or an apple. Do you have any treats of that kind?"

"Of course," said Joseph as Hattie moved to the side of Maximus with his crutch. "We often—oh."

He had slipped from his stallion's back but entirely misjudged it. Suddenly, he was pressed up between Maximus's side and Hattie's chest, her hands on each side to balance him.

And his hands—his hands were on her hips.

Perhaps that's what made him do it. Joseph wasn't thinking clearly as it was, the euphoria of having made progress a powerful intoxication—but this was more.

Being so close to Hattie, feeling her breasts rise and fall against his chest, feeling the warmth of her through her hips—

It had been so long. Painfully long since he had held a woman.

Joseph dipped his head and claimed a kiss from the woman he had, only weeks ago, declared could teach him nothing.

For a moment, Hattie shied away, but within a heartbeat, she stayed still. Joseph could not help himself, tilting her head to deepen the kiss, and she let him.

And oh, she felt wonderful. She tasted glorious, warm and silky in his arms. Waves of pleasure rushed through his chest—

Hattie backed away and Joseph almost fell. Was that the lack of a crutch, or the swimming dizziness of the kiss?

"I—I didn't expect—"

"I am sorry," Joseph said gruffly. "My mistake. It won't happen again."

He had started stomping back to the house before Hattie could say a word. It had been a mistake. Certainly not one he would repeat.

Except, perhaps, all night in his dreams.

Chapter Six

December 4, 1810

HATTIE TOOK A long, deep breath.

"You, Harriet Godwin, are being ridiculous," she said firmly to her reflection. "Thinking about that kiss is the absolute last thing you should be doing. You have a job to do. You have money to earn! So I order you to stop thinking about it right…now!"

Her gaze met her own glare, and she felt the fury. The fury against herself.

If only it were that easy. If only she could simply force herself to stop thinking about the most incredible, the most sensual…

"I—I didn't expect—"

"I am sorry. My mistake. It won't happen again."

Hattie swallowed. One kiss from a gentleman who was perennially furious should not make her feel this way. One kiss that was evidently a complete mistake, a reflex of a duke that appeared to know no better, was nothing to hold onto.

It certainly wasn't any excuse to get what her mother would have called "ideas."

But she had.

What woman wouldn't? The Duke of Wincham was handsome, irritable, tall, dark…

Hattie had met plenty of men over the years. There were always farmhands about, stable lads when she could afford them. There were men in the village she had known since she was a small child. The vicar, Reverend McKee, had christened her as an infant.

None of them made her feel…like this.

Like her own heart was going to burst out of her chest. As though she couldn't breathe when merely thinking about him.

"You are his horse trainer," Hattie told her reflection sternly. "And nothing more."

That was the truth. Try as she might, losing herself completely in her own imagination, Hattie could not conceive of a situation in which Wincham—*the Duke of Wincham!*—would consider her as anything but an inconvenience who knew her way around horses.

That was not why she was there, Hattie told herself firmly, piling up her hair into a bun and securing it with a ribbon and several pins. She was being paid, and most generously, to help the man learn to ride again.

And that was all.

Besides, she knew what could happen if she allowed herself to get foolish ideas. No one in the area knew of that engagement—that failed engagement, she thought bitterly. And she wished to keep it that way. No one had to know.

Hattie breathed in the cold wintery air as she strode across to her stables. Bramble was eagerly awaiting her, stamping in the freezing morning, impatient to be free.

A smile finally crept across Hattie's face. "I know, we'll be out soon."

There was something marvelous about riding across fields and fen in the early days of winter. Hattie had smelled the frost on the air two days ago, knew it was coming. Everyone who lived in the country, who truly knew it, had seen it coming.

But that hadn't diminished its beauty when it had finally

arrived.

Frost pricked out the elegant curves of the leaves still hanging onto the tall beech trees that lined the only three fields still remaining to Godwin Place. It highlighted the shimmery shine of the berries in the hedgerows, birds flocking to them, pecking hungrily. And the frost carved out her mare's horseshoe prints behind her as Hattie cantered across the fields.

Oh, there was nothing like this!

Hattie couldn't remember the first time she had ridden a horse. It was as obvious as breathing, as easy as walking. Sometimes she wondered how long she could go without her own feet touching the ground.

It was why, even after several more lessons, she would not permit Wincham to simply give up.

If she could help him return to that wonderful feeling, if he could reclaim with her assistance the ability to go riding again, to feel this brilliant rush of excitement…

Well, all the difficulty would be worth it.

The Wincham stable yard was busy as ever when Hattie pulled Bramble to a trot.

"Morning, Miss Hattie," said Mr. Knowles, tugging his forelock.

Hattie nodded in turn. "Mr. Knowles."

There had been an element of frostiness between them when she had first been invited—*well, ordered*—to teach a few lessons on Wincham's land.

It was to be expected, Hattie had told herself. Mr. Knowles had his own way of doing things, his own expectations of his horses. He wouldn't want her to change things, no doubt.

She certainly wouldn't want a man turning up at her stables, ordering her about.

But she had gradually, Hattie assumed, earned his respect. He wasn't watching her so closely anyway, which almost meant the same thing.

"His Grace is not out yet," Mr. Knowles said quietly. "Perhaps if ye would like a cuppa tea—"

"I'm here, I'm here," came a grumpy voice. "No need to assume I'll always be late. I can walk almost as well as you, you know."

Hattie stifled a smile as she shared a look with Mr. Knowles. If there was one thing she liked about the stablehand, it was that he knew how to handle his master.

"Never doubted ye for a moment, Y'Grace," said Mr. Knowles. "I'll leave you to it."

She watched him go, allowing her gaze to linger on him just a little longer than she would have done. Anything to keep herself from looking at—

"You, on the other hand, are late," said Wincham gruffly.

With her heart leaping, Hattie turned to the duke. He was glaring, as though she had committed some terrible crime.

"I was out here in the stable yard before you," she pointed out calmly.

As though her heart was roaring in her chest. As though her fingers weren't tingling. As though her hips weren't aching to be held by him again.

How was he doing it, this gruff and ill-mannered duke? Even when she hadn't known who he was, there'd been something different about him. Something about the way he'd glared, as though everything in the world was someone else's fault, and when he discovered who—

"Well?" said Wincham with a raised eyebrow. "Don't tell me we're continuing with mounting again."

Hattie allowed herself a small smile. "And what would you do if I said we were?"

It was just a hint of a tease, but enough to stoke the fires in her chest.

Wincham was tired of it, she knew. He wanted to be riding, properly riding. Cantering over his land, perusing his tenants, returning to the life he once had.

But Hattie knew better than most that if he were truly to feel comfortable again on a horse, truly at one with his mount, he had to learn the hard way. Even if he didn't like it.

"At least that damned mounting block is gone," Wincham muttered as Mr. Knowles brought out Maximus.

Hattie looked about. Now that he came to mention it… "Yes, where is it?"

He had progressed well the last few lessons, now able to mount Maximus from the very first step. Today, she had promised, they would start practicing mounting from the ground. The first thing he had wished to do. The first step to reclaiming his confidence.

Wincham met her eyes. "I had it burned."

"You—you had it—"

"To ashes," said Wincham crisply. "I never want to see that damned thing again."

Hattie could not help but stare as Maximus stood before her and Mr. Knowles returned to the stables.

He'd…he'd had it burned?

What sort of a man was this duke, who took it upon himself to destroy what he then conquered? How could she think to trust him as a man, not a client, if this was how he behaved?

"I will admit, it did my soul good to see it go up in flames," continued the duke with a wry grin. "Something very cathartic about seeing it go. I've got one of my carpenters making a new one, obviously. A new start."

And a rush of sympathy, or pride, or something else cascaded through Hattie's body so swiftly it almost made her gasp.

He was not then the destructive, bitter man she had supposed. No, this was a man who recognized the end of seasons and the beginning of new ones. Who recognized his dependence on things and yet allowed his temper to burn brightly.

He was still having a new mounting block made.

"Hattie?"

Hattie's cheeks burned as she met Wincham's gaze. Despite telling him he could speak to her using her nickname, she wasn't sure anymore whether that was a good idea. Something stirred in her whenever his lips curled around her name.

"Yes?"

"Are we to begin?"

"We…we are indeed," said Hattie, trying to collect herself and reaching up to pat Maximus's neck. "Ready, boy?"

The stallion snuffled, blowing in her face.

Hattie grinned. There was something about horses she just never saw in men. A kindness. A softness, an awareness of their own strength yet knowledge of when to use it.

She readied herself. "So, we're moving on to mounting from the ground. As you'll remember, when mounting from the first step you had to carefully swing your arm…"

It was easy to lose herself in training. That was what Hattie knew; it came to her like breathing. Where others had to struggle and strain to understand, it came naturally to her. She didn't have to strive for it.

Not like Wincham.

Hattie watched, transfixed, as the man stood beside the horse. He was breathing slowly, his eyes unfocused, as he attempted to prepare his body for something he had once told her was impossible.

It was impossible not to admire the man. Others would speak over her, assume as a woman she could not possibly know what she was talking about.

But Wincham?

"Here we go," he breathed.

Hattie knew the moment he moved that he would not make it. Not enough swing in the arms. But she allowed him to attempt it, allowed him to see just how high up Maximus's side he was able to get his leg.

And watched as he fell to the cobblestones.

It was not pleasant. Her heart wrenched as Wincham's curse echoed around the stable. But she had to let him try, and fail. How else would the man learn?

Wincham managed to stand, face clouded with anger. "Y'see, it's impossible!"

"It's not impossible," Hattie said calmly.

"You think so?" snarled Wincham. "And what makes you so sure of that?"

"Because," Hattie said, her heart thundering but knowing she was speaking the truth. "Because when I first met you—"

"Yes, remind me of how helpless I am, how weak," snapped the duke, turning away. "Remind me how I couldn't get up without help—"

"And now you have."

Hattie watched as Wincham turned slowly to look back at her, his face amazed.

"What…what did you say?"

She pointed to the ground. "You just fell, Wincham, and you got up. Without your crutch. Without any help. Without even thinking about it."

In a way, she was proud. Hattie knew it was thanks to her careful gait training that Wincham had his balance back, that he could move more smoothly and swiftly through the air.

Even if he didn't realize it.

He was realizing it now. Wincham looked at the ground in astonishment, then at his crutch propped up against a stable wall.

"I…I did, didn't I?" he said in wonder.

Hattie grinned as her stomach swooped. Why did it mean so much to her to see him succeed? "So. Ready to try again?"

The duke did not reply. At least, not in words.

Ignoring her completely, he twisted to get in position beside Maximus. Hattie watched as he concentrated, trying to feel all of his body before he moved, as she had taught him, not during the movement itself.

Hattie's gaze was drawn to the knot in his breeches just below his left knee. It would take months for his true new balance to be gained, but then…

As she had known he would the moment he moved, Wincham did not manage to mount his horse.

"Damn and blast it, the thing's impossible!" he snapped, managing to stop himself from falling to the ground by grasping onto Maximus, who shook his head.

Hattie took a deep breath. "I know it seems difficult—"

"I said I cannot do it, and I speak advisedly," Wincham said, glaring. "I know myself, I know my limits, and—"

And that was when Hattie lost her temper.

It had been awhile coming. Oh, the many lessons she had given the Duke of Wincham had been absolutely packed full of him losing his temper. There didn't seem to be five minutes together in which the gentleman did not glare, or curse, or mutter under his breath.

And she had been patient. You had to be, working with men. Horses were patient of their own accord, most of them, but men?

Hattie had enough of being grumbled at. She may be being paid, true, but she was still a lady. She was determined to be treated like it.

"You know absolutely nothing!" Hattie snapped. "For goodness sake, man, I've already proved to you time and time again! With practice and instruction, I can get you to do almost anything!"

Wincham stared, evidently outraged. "You can't speak to me like that!"

"I'll speak to you how I want!" Hattie said, her voice and temper rising.

It was a mistake. It was certainly not ladylike. Hattie knew she would lose all good standing in the man's eyes after her outburst, but in this moment, blood boiling, she didn't care.

Why should she have to pander to a man's pathetic tantrums when she had more important things to do in her own stables? Why did she have to listen to this complaining when she had already done so much for him?

"You're not teaching me properly," snarled Wincham, pointing a finger. "I should have asked a man to teach a man's work!"

Fury curled around Hattie's heart. It was the same all over! Why did men think they were the only ones able to have a serious thought in their bones!

"I'm doing my best and I'm doing it well," Hattie continued furiously as Wincham continued to stare as though she had sprouted another head. "I think I'm the best horse trainer around here, but I'm not a governess! I can't teach a man manners, and though you sorely need it, I don't seem to have the power to force some sense into you."

"Sense, into me!" Wincham looked genuinely outraged. "I'm not the one marching about in breeches when you should be in a gown! I'm not the one—"

"I'm trying to help you, you idiot, and if you had any sense, you'd listen to me!" shot back Hattie.

This was all going wrong. This was a disaster. Though she knew she should stop, apologize, hope the man would still pay her the fifty pounds, Hattie could not stop herself.

All the frustration she had kept bottled up for so long was pouring out of her and it just happened that Wincham was the man in the way.

"I don't want help," said the duke curtly. "I'm never offered help."

Hattie took a deep breath, but her anger continued to flow. "Well I'm not surprised, if this is how you treat people! Do you ever wonder why you've been alone in that big manor of yours for so long?"

It was perhaps not the right thing to say, but she could not help but point it out. No family, few guests, the man was completely alone. Had he pushed everyone away as he was trying to push her away?

Though horror sparked in her chest at how blunt she was being, Hattie knew it was too late. Wincham was staring, astonishment clear in his eyes.

Well, she'd gone this far.

"You're going to have to accept you can't get things perfect on the first go," snapped Hattie with a glare. "So swallow the bitter pill and put your best foot forward!"

For a heartbeat, just a heartbeat, Hattie froze.

Well, that had done it.

"Or leg, or whatever," she amended hastily, her cheeks burning. "Oh hell—"

"I know what you meant," Wincham said quietly.

Hattie swallowed. The look of incredulous irritation was gone. Now the man was looking like…

Well. She wasn't entirely sure. Certainly not how he had been looking at her before.

"Right," she said helplessly.

Was that…was that a smile on the duke's face? "Do you feel better now?"

Hattie tried to take a breath and found the constriction in her chest was gone. "Yes," she admitted with a dry laugh. "Much better. You?"

"Ten times better, I suppose," he said with a shrug. "Dear God, you have a temper on you, don't you?"

Shoulders tensed, Hattie waited for the criticism. It always followed a comment of that kind. Whenever her temper, her boldness, her inability to act as society expected a young lady to act, overwhelmed her, she was given the lecture.

That's not what ladies do. That's not what ladies say. That's not what ladies—

"Well, better to have things out in the open, I say," said Wincham unexpectedly.

Hattie blinked. "I…I beg your pardon?"

The duke sighed, and somehow the pity she'd felt ever since she'd realized his leg was missing changed. It wasn't absent as such. Merely…different. Warmer. Softer.

"I'm not the sort of man to let things fester," he said quietly. "I speak my mind, and I speak how I find. It hasn't earned me many friends."

Hattie smiled nervously. "I think we're alike in that regard."

And the sunshine broke through the clouds, transforming the stable yard. The frost that licked along the stone walls, the roofs, came alight, glowing and sparkling.

When Hattie looked back at Wincham, he was smiling.

"I was wrong. Can you forgive me?"

"Of course," she said instantly. She was hardly one to hold a grudge.

Wincham's eyes sparkled in the sunlight. "Aren't you going to apologize?"

"I don't regret a thing I said," shot back Hattie with another laugh. "Now, try again. I've got to be back on my farm in an hour."

The duke looked as though he was going to say something, but he evidently thought better of it. Instead, he shifted his attention to the horse beside him.

Hattie watched as Wincham attempted, and once again failed, to mount Maximus.

"Another failure closer to success," she heard him mutter.

It was hard not to respect a man who said things like that. "And again."

Chapter Seven

December 6, 1810

IT HAD BEEN weeks since Joseph had ridden through this part of the Wincham Forest. Or was it months?

It certainly felt that long. The trees had completely changed. Their summer color had faded to autumnal gold then completely disappeared, falling to the ground to become part of the mulch.

Joseph looked around in wonder. How had he never noticed how beautiful this place was?

"I've never been along this path."

He glanced to his left as his heart skipped a beat.

Hattie Godwin. The woman was fast becoming the only person he wanted to see, her brash honesty the only palatable conversation. How had that happened?

It had probably begun, Joseph thought, after that argument.

"I don't want help. I'm never offered help."

"Well I'm not surprised, if this is how you treat people! Do you ever wonder why you've been alone in that big manor of yours for so long?"

Not his finest moment, in truth, but he had never been known for his calm or measured manner. He spoke without a filter, without any propriety holding him back, and it showed.

Strangely, Hattie had responded in kind. She had spoken

bluntly, laying out his faults for the world to see, and Joseph had found, much to his displeasure, that he did not like them.

And the only way to change that was to change himself.

Well, not completely. His attitude, certainly. On that point, she had been correct. Joseph had never thought about it that way, but she was right. He had pushed people away, or ensured they could not come too close. No invitations to Cedarworth Lacey had been issued since his injury. The Martocks had been swiftly put back on the road. The only people he had seen regularly were his servants and his doctor.

Not exactly the conversational excellence he was accustomed to. No offense to Knowles.

But since then, Joseph had worked hard to…well, not self-censure. He didn't want to become a different person. Just…just the person that Hattie wanted him to be.

He pushed the thought aside as the path curved around to the right, the soft muffled clopping of their mounts' hooves the only sound in the wintery forest.

Joseph Chisholm, Duke of Wincham, was not going to utterly transform his character merely to receive the approbation of a young miss!

Even if she was that beautiful!

"This is all Wincham land, isn't it?"

Joseph nodded, glad for the excuse to look at Hattie again. "Yes, it has been in our family for generations. My father always said William the Conqueror gave it to us as thanks for our prowess in battle."

Hattie raised an unimpressed eyebrow. "And you believed him?"

He chuckled, shaking his head. "Not really."

She grinned then turned to look ahead. Joseph was afforded the opportunity to have a proper look at the woman riding alongside him.

She was…well. Not the sort of woman he had expected.

The breeches were still present, of course. Joseph wondered

again if he would recognize Miss Hattie Godwin if she were not wearing them. Today's were a light musky brown, curving sensuously over her—

Joseph forced his gaze further up. Her riding habit was that of a man's, hiding the exquisite curves he had felt in that reckless moment he had kissed her. Her dark hair was pinned up once more, tightly restrained.

Quite opposite to her character, in fact…

"You're learning too far to the left."

Joseph started. Hattie was examining him with a professional eye, not the adoring one he had just been imagining.

He shook his head as though ridding his ears of water. As though that could dislodge the thoughts he'd been having…

"The left, you're leaning too far over," repeated Hattie, pointing. "See?"

Joseph nodded, adjusting himself in the saddle. He did not bother to explain the reason was because he had found him unconsciously, then consciously, wishing to be closer to her.

Not the sort of thing a gentleman should admit. Let alone a duke.

"Is that better?" Joseph asked stiffly.

He shouldn't have asked, really. He had only done so because he was so eager for her gaze on him, to feel the caressing look of—

He was being ridiculous, Joseph told himself sternly as their horses walked slowly along the path. Hattie—Miss Godwin, as he should probably consider her—had absolutely no interest in a duke down on his luck. She certainly didn't want to be around a man who constantly complained, had bitter nightmares, and had stolen a kiss.

Heat tinged Joseph's cheeks as Hattie's proficient eye scanned him.

"That's better," she said with a nod. "See here, the way your stirrup is long on that side?"

Joseph's stomach churned as he looked at his left stirrup.

Knowles had asked him about it when he had been tacking up the horses before today's ride. "I don't have to put a stirrup on the left, Y'Grace, it'll only dangle—"

"You put that stirrup on like you would for another other man," Joseph had snarled. "And I never want to have this discussion again."

Queasiness settled in his stomach as a woodpecker flew out before him and Hattie. "I…I asked Knowles to put it on. Even though it's useless."

When he glanced at his riding companion, it was to see her wry look.

"Asked. You mean told."

Joseph nodded with a shrug. "I suppose so."

He had never considered there to be a difference before. Knowles was a servant; Joseph didn't have to ask anything of his servants. He mentioned something, and it was done. That was the way it always had been.

"You didn't think to remove it?"

"I don't want anything different. No special treatment."

It had been one of the first arguments he'd had with Doctor Walsingham. When he had insisted on some sort of bath chair, and—

"Why do I get the feeling that you've had this argument before?" Hattie's voice was soft, but it still contained the same steel with which she always spoke.

It had been her idea to take this trail, and he had been grateful. He'd wanted nothing more than to ride out here, anywhere. Feel the shift of his horse beneath him. Feel one with the ground, feel like he was floating through the air.

Somehow, she had known that within him, even if he had not expressed it.

And she had sensed this, too. How did she do it? How did the woman seem to know what he was thinking even before he understood it himself?

He sighed as the forest thinned out into a glade where weak

wintery sunshine poured down.

"When the stump—when I was first healed," Joseph said, hating the word, hating that he'd said it, "my doctor—"

"Doctor Walsingham."

"Am I telling this story or are you?" he said in a heartbeat.

For a moment, Joseph was sure he'd gone too far. It was all very well to speak like that to chaps at the Dulverton Club, but to a lady? Even a lady in breeches?

Hattie grinned. "I deserved that. Go on."

Joseph relaxed, settling once more into his saddle. The imbalance in his limbs, one foot in a saddle, and his stump just resting against the side of Maximus, grated once more.

"Doctor Walsingham wanted me to get me into some sort of bath chair," he said with a dark glower.

There was a moment's pause. And then—

"And that was a problem…because?" Hattie asked lightly.

Wasn't it obvious? "I told you, I don't need adjustments. I want to be treated like any—"

"Tell me, where do you get your breeches?" interrupted Hattie once again.

Joseph frowned as their two horses meandered leisurely into a denser part of the forest, the trees enclosing over them again.

Breeches? What had breeches got to do with it?

"Don't tell me you want the name of my tailor," he said, trying to jest. "I think the ones you have already suit you very well."

Despite his better judgment, Joseph allowed his gaze to slip to her buttocks.

There was a sharp intake of breath. It wasn't his.

"I merely meant," said Hattie. Joseph dragged his gaze to her face and saw her cheeks were as red as his. "When you go to a tailor, he uses your measurements, does he not?"

He could not see precisely what she was getting at. "Of course."

"Because it would be madness to attempt to fit you with a

pair of breeches designed for someone else," Hattie said quietly.

Joseph still couldn't understand what she was trying to prove. "Yes, so—"

"You could almost say," she said with a grin, "he was making an adjustment."

He stared. His stomach twisted as the truth of her words, the elegance of her point, soared into his mind, demonstrating just how idiotic he was.

Well, he should have expected it. Hattie had proven countless times she was far wittier than many of his friends. She'd be running rings around Martock, and as for Chantmarle—

"Fine, fine, I see your point," Joseph said gruffly, trying to ignore the swell of awe in his chest. "You're saying that everyone has things adjusted for them, even small things."

"If something as simple as breeches can be adjusted, then why not everything?" Hattie said with a shrug. "Here."

"What are you—?"

"Just hold still, will you?" Hattie said matter-of-factly as she dismounted.

Joseph drew Maximus to a halt, his heart hammering. What was she doing?

He watched as the horse trainer stepped around her own mare and toward his mount.

"Hie there, Maximus," Hattie said quietly, patting the stallion on the nose.

Heat was flowing through Joseph's body as she approached his left side. It wasn't just Hattie's presence, although that was more than enough to raise his temperature.

No, it was that his stump, a part of him he assiduously hid at every opportunity, was, thanks to Maximus's height, right at her eye line.

Joseph swallowed. The knot in his breeches hid it completely, of course, but it still made him feel incredibly vulnerable. No one had ever touched it, even through clothes, save for Doctor Walsingham. He'd ceased allowing his valet into his dressing room when Joseph was having a bath, for fear of the man seeing it.

And now Hattie was reaching out a hand—

"Don't mind me," she said cheerfully.

Joseph flinched as her deft fingers pushed his knee back to reach the stirrup.

And…nothing happened.

He wasn't entirely sure what he had expected. The world to collapse, perhaps. Fire to rain down from the heavens. He certainly thought the world would end in some fashion, the earth maybe swallowing him up.

But all that happened was a rather pleasant tingle rushing up his knee and to his loins, stirring something that had been allowed to stay dormant for quite some time.

Joseph cleared his throat. This was not the time to be thinking about that!

He lifted his gaze and looked around them, hoping to distract himself from the strange jerks and tugs on his saddle as Hattie did something to his stirrup. This was all ridiculous, of course. He should never have permitted her to talk to him about such a nonsensical thing as—

"There," said Hattie firmly with a sense of pride in her voice. "See?"

Joseph did not particularly want to see. However, he recalled the words she had shot at him only days before.

"I don't want help. I'm never offered help."

"Well I'm not surprised, if this is how you treat people!"

Was this not the ideal opportunity to demonstrate to Hattie he could accept help?

And so suppressing his urge to complain, Joseph looked down.

And blinked. He could not be seeing that correctly.

Somehow, and he would have to ask her another time precisely how she had done it, Hattie had adjusted his stirrup by at least a foot. It was much higher up on Maximus's back now, at a height he would not have believed possible. It looked more like the stirrup of a child than a man.

Discomfort stirred in his heart. "Well I don't see what that's supposed to—"

"You really are dense sometimes, you do know that?" said Hattie conversationally.

Joseph opened his mouth, ready to share his outrage. "How dare you—"

And he halted. His heart was still thundering in his chest, his head felt it was on fire, and for an instant, he wanted to scream into the world that nothing was fair.

But Joseph managed to swallow it. He looked into Hattie's eyes, her uncomplicated patience, and knew he wanted to be a better man.

For her.

Hattie's lips curled into a gentle smile. "Look at this."

Her words were soft and her touch was the same. Joseph forced himself not to flinch as Hattie reached out and took his knee in her hand. She pulled it forward inch by inch and slotted his stump into the stirrup.

Joseph blinked. "Dear God."

Now why hadn't he thought of that?

It was so obvious, now that she had done it. Why, this way, he would have even greater control of the beast beneath him. It would be easier to stay balanced, easier to instruct Maximus with just the nudges of his legs where he wanted to go.

And she had managed it in just a few minutes?

"Th-Thank you," Joseph stammered, hating the weakness in his voice but knowing he had to say something. "Thank you, Hattie."

Their gazes met. Joseph longed to lean down and kiss her. Taste her again, know the wonder of having her close.

Thankfully, the swift imbalance this would cause was enough to hold him back.

Hattie's cheeks were pinking. "It is a small thing."

"No, it is not," Joseph said emphatically. "It is a great thing. Thank you."

She still looked embarrassed as she released his knee and started walking back to her mare. "Sometimes it takes someone else to look at a problem and see how it could be fixed."

"You are certainly more intelligent than any of my stable-hands," Joseph said dryly. "Knowles will have a fit when he sees it."

Was that a flicker of triumph in her eyes?

He could have been mistaken. The weak winter sunlight flickered strangely here underneath the bare branches. But Joseph was almost certain Hattie had been celebratory at his words.

His heart sank. Was that all this was? A game, a competition between Knowles and Hattie Godwin as to who could get him on a horse quicker? Was this professional pride, and not something more, that kept drawing her closer?

"I'm just glad you're finally listening to me," said Hattie with a grin as she mounted.

Joseph's jaw dropped. "What do you mean?"

"I think that's the first time I've said something or done something outlandish, and you've just let me get on and do it," she pointed out, nudging her horse forward.

Joseph wanted to argue as he nudged Maximus forward also. The trouble was, he didn't have much ground to stand on, and he was usually shaky on the ground with Hattie at best.

"Am I really that bad?"

Hattie could evidently hear his rueful tone, for her smile broadened. "Definitely."

Warmth rushed through Joseph as he chuckled, shaking his head as their two horses started to walk again along the forest path.

There was something about this woman. Oh, he'd met plenty of ladies in town. Almack's was full of them, as were Lady Romeril's card parties. Hyde Park, St James's Park, every street always seemed to be crammed with ladies.

All the same. All dull.

But not Hattie. She was different. She surprised him and that was a relief after being alone for so long. And the way she kissed—

"So, tell me," said Hattie quietly, breaking the silence. "How did it happen?"

Joseph stiffened. "I lost part of my leg."

His tone attempted to convey, in the way his words could not, that he had absolutely no wish to speak of it. *Who would?* The traumatic moment had been bad enough to live through, and to suffer through again and again in his nightmares. The last thing he wanted to do was recount it.

"Well, I rather gathered that," said Hattie quietly, pushing an escaped lock of hair behind her ear. "I wondered how."

Joseph glared, all calm forgotten in the face of such questioning. *How dare she!*

As though she could hear his thoughts, Hattie's cheeks colored. "I know it is none of my business. I am a curious creature, though, and—"

"You would ask something like that?" Joseph said quietly, trying to keep bitterness from his tone. "Of me?"

"Does being a duke make you special?" she shot back.

It was on the tip of tongue to say yes. *Of course it does*, Joseph wanted to say. He was different. His whole life was different to most people. Usually for the better, but in this case, for the worse.

Was he to become some spectacle for the locals?

"I wouldn't ask just anyone, you know," came Hattie's quiet words. "But as you are the only gentleman I have…who has…I mean…"

Joseph's heart skipped a beat.

Dear God, was she trying to say he was the only gentleman who had ever kissed her?

Surely not. With those looks, that charm, and those breeches, Joseph was certain Hattie had been fighting men off with a stick. There must be countless gentlemen in the area that had made overtures to her.

Which did not explain, he realized, why she was still unmarried.

Joseph swallowed as he tried not to notice the tense way Hattie was carrying herself, all that natural calm lost.

It was difficult not to feel possessive. The first man who had tasted those lips, who knew what it was to have Hattie pressed against him…

"I thought it would help," came Hattie's quiet voice. "If you talked about it."

And a great churning pain lurched in Joseph's stomach.

Talk about it? *Talk about it?* He could barely look at it, even all after these months. What good would it do to talk about the damned thing?

Joseph glanced over at Hattie and, for a moment, the pain seemed to lessen. Perhaps, if he could bring himself to uncover even more of his pain—

But the instinct fell away. He couldn't do it. He would not speak of it, never.

"I don't want to talk about it," Joseph said quietly.

He had been certain Hattie would push the point—she certainly had no compunction in pushing other demands of hers.

But as her dark eyes met his, there was a flash of understanding. How, Joseph could not tell. But for a moment, he felt she understood what it was to feel this…this empty.

"I understand," Hattie said quietly. "And I am here to talk if that ever changes."

Joseph nodded curtly, not trusting his tongue. They settled into silence, listening only to the soft muffled thumps of their horses' hooves, and the cry of a woodpecker echoing through the trees.

Chapter Eight

December 11, 1810

"It was just a suggestion," Hattie said quietly.

Her stomach was twisting into knots and she couldn't precisely put her finger on why. Wincham didn't need to speak for her to know what was on his mind. It was painted on his face.

They had met outside her stables, as agreed. The morning air was freezing, the clouds overcast and heavy. Thanks to her father's thick riding coat and the leather gloves she had slipped on that morning, Hattie was warm enough, though her breath billowed on the breeze.

The Duke of Wincham was even more finely dressed but far less comfortable.

"I am not entirely…I had not considered that. Not yet," he said quietly.

Hattie's gaze raked over his face, seeing the telltale expressions of hesitancy she was starting to recognize.

He was a strange one, this duke. At times forceful and angry, at others shy, vulnerable.

If someone had told her, when she had first encountered—*no, argued*—with the Duke of Wincham that he could be quiet and unsure, she would have laughed in their face and sent them packing.

But as the days slipped by, Hattie was seeing more and more of him. He was opening to her, even if he did not know it.

"Riding over to the ridge?" Wincham's jaw tightened. "I haven't been there since…"

He didn't need to finish the sentence. "Since you were injured, yes, I thought so."

"It's dangerous terrain out there, especially in winter," Wincham said, glancing over his shoulder in the direction of the hills. "If something was to happen—I mean…it's not like I could walk back."

There was such stiffness, such discomfort in his words that, for a moment, Hattie was tempted to give up the suggestion.

She had made it carefully, assessing his progress the last few days. From what she could see, Wincham had grown in confidence with each passing hour on a horse. Maximus was gentle with him, despite his great size, and now that Wincham had two stirrups he could use, he was starting to control the beast rather than allow Maximus to wend where he wished.

But that didn't change the last few months.

"You are right," said Hattie quietly, pushing back a wayward curl. "Perhaps it is too difficult for you."

The moment Wincham met her eyes, she knew she'd said the right thing. "I didn't say I couldn't do it."

Hattie shrugged. "There's no shame in it—"

"I just think one should be cautious," he said, speaking over her. "It would never do to take unnecessary risks just because one hadn't considered everything, thought it through."

It was all she could do to nod while keeping a straight face. "To be sure. Plenty of people would not consider themselves competent enough for such a trail. I quite understand."

Hattie stood, watching with gentle mirth, which she ensured did not show on her face, as the man wrestled with himself.

It was a low trick. Her father would have said it was teasing, something a genteel young lady should never consider, let alone do. The trouble was men were so easily manipulated. A few clever words, a subtle raise of the eyebrows, a shrug, and it was done.

And the poor things were never the wiser.

She should be careful, Hattie knew. One day she was going to find she couldn't sway a man like that, and she would actually have to try to persuade him. *Heaven forbid.*

"Well, I have considered everything, and I think we go," said Wincham smartly. "Now. If—if that suits you, of course, Hattie."

Heat suffused Hattie's cheeks as she met his gaze. "O-Of course."

Why was it in that moment, despite her complete control of the conversation, that control began to slip? How did he look at her that way, with a gaze unremarkable in others, that made her whole body quiver, unsure precisely where she was or what she was saying?

Flickers of anticipation, of longing, rushed through her. Hattie was conscious they were standing only feet apart. Just a few inches between their fingertips…

"You don't have to be afraid," Wincham said quietly.

Hattie swallowed. How on earth did he do that? Know what she was thinking?

"I-I'm not," she breathed.

How had she become closer to him? Had she stepped forward, or had he?

Hattie couldn't tell, but she did know his lips were closer now. His mouth nearing hers. Her heart was pattering, increasing in pace, shortening her breath, making her think—

"Because if something happens, I'll protect you," Wincham said, his gaze blazing.

Hattie swallowed. She was not going to think about kissing Wincham. She was not about to kiss the Duke of—

She was not going to kiss a duke!

Hattie lurched backward. "Right! Right, in that case, I shall prepare my mare. Maximus looks ready—are you ready? Be ready."

And without explaining herself in any capacity, Hattie strode quickly over to the stable door, threw it open, and stepped through.

In the quiet, warm, uncomplicated stable, she tried to draw a long and deep breath.

What on earth had gotten into her?

She was not normally the sort of idiot girl to start fawning over a man just because he was handsome. And kind. And noble.

Hattie shook her head. *Harriet Godwin!*

She was just getting caught up in the romance, she tried to tell herself. Not that there was any romance between them! It was more…well. A romantic idea. The injured duke, horse riding, a wintery setting…

It was easy to lose one's common sense in such a situation, Hattie thought firmly as she moved to tack up her favorite mare.

But she wasn't here to—to attract a duke's affection! She was here to train him and his horse. And that was all. He was paying her, she was essentially a servant!

And with that thought, Hattie's shoulders slumped and all the excitement at being so close to Wincham melted away.

It was true. She was just as much a servant to him as Mr. Knowles, or Mrs. Alan, or any one of the hundreds of servants who worked in Cedarworth Lacey. They were paid by him, ordered about by him, and were probably viewed by Wincham as nothing more.

"And that's all you are, my girl," Hattie muttered to her mare as she buckled on the saddle carefully. "Just a—"

"Do you always talk to your horse?"

Hattie whirled around. Just how long had Wincham been standing there?

"Of course," she said as airily as she could manage. "Some of the most sensible conversations I have are with horses."

For a moment, just a moment, he stared as though she was utterly mad. Then his lips quirked into a smile.

"I find that true as well," Wincham said quietly. "Well. Are you ready?"

Hattie nodded. As ready as she would ever be.

The trouble was, swiftly pulling herself up into saddle once Bramble had been led outside, that "ready" was not something Hattie had ever been lacking.

She understood the stud farm. Knew the breeding lines, knew what qualities people looked for in their animals. Until the last year or so, when unexpected bills arrived, she had managed to keep the place afloat.

But this? Conversations with a duke? Now that was something she'd never prepared for…

"I used to love this trail," said Wincham quietly as they left her farm and headed toward the hills.

Hattie smiled, the tension in her neck disappearing as the conversation focused on the beauty of nature around them. "It's one of my favorites, I think. I used to come up here when I was younger, when I wasn't wanted around the farm and considered a nuisance inside."

"What—you used to ride up here all alone?"

Hattie chuckled to see the astonishment on his face. "You think I was foolhardy?"

"I am surprised you were not injured," said the duke candidly as the terrain started to slope upward. "It can be a dangerous path, if you do not know what you are doing."

It was a fair comment—in most cases. "Yet I have always known what I am doing."

"Always?"

Hattie shivered. She had glanced at her riding companion at the very moment he had spoken, and there was a look in his eye…

Something she had not seen in the man's face before.

"Look, Wincham—"

"Joseph."

Hattie blinked. Something churned in her stomach, but the

sensation was not unpleasant. "Joseph?"

The Duke of Wincham shrugged. "It's my name. It seems odd to be calling you Hattie with you calling me by my title. You don't mind, do you?"

Hattie swallowed. *What a question to ask!*

On the one hand, it was perfectly logical. As their horses softly treaded up the path, snorting at times, their breath billowing, Hattie could see the man's point. He called her by her first name. Why not afford her the same privilege?

But on the other hand, and this one was far more obvious, Hattie knew she could never speak to a duke with such intimacy! Where would it all end?

She firmly pushed away the sensual suggestion that her mind immediately provided. *Not there!*

"Absolutely not," she said decisively.

It appeared the duke had not expected such a robust response. "I beg your pardon?"

"You are a duke—the Duke of Wincham; you own half the county!" Hattie tried not to think about it. *Dear lord…* "I could just as easily call you Your Highness as…as Joseph."

Even saying the name without directly addressing him felt wrong. Hattie's head spun as they moved into a forested part of the trail, climbing higher with every horse's step.

Wincham shrugged. "I'm asking you, though. It would be a kindness to me. I…well, I almost never get to hear my own name spoken, isn't that funny?"

Despite herself, Hattie was curious. "What do you mean?"

The duke nudged Maximus closer to her mare, and she did not give Bramble a nudge to take a similar step away. It felt…right. Him being this close.

"Well, my servants call me Your Grace, and friends, when I see them, call me Wincham, and that's about it," the man said easily. "I haven't heard myself called Joseph in many a year. It's strange to have a name no one uses."

Hattie considered this as the tender silence was broken by a robin singing out his heart somewhere in the trees around them.

To never hear one's name.

It was not something she could easily understand. She had been Hattie for so long to almost everyone she sometimes forgot she was supposed to be "Miss Godwin" in company. Miss Godwin sounded like someone's maiden aunt, she thought wryly. Who drank too much sherry and muttered about the good old days—

"Now, what are you thinking of?"

Hattie started, trying to dissemble as she caught his eye. "Nothing, it was nothing—"

"I know you were thinking of something amusing, Hattie, so don't try to tell me otherwise," Joseph said sternly.

Hattie blinked. She'd thought of him as Joseph.

Oh, bother.

"I was just thinking how…how we are so different in that regard," she said. "I am always Hattie; the idea of being 'Miss Godwin' is a strange one. Yet it is the opposite for you."

Joseph nodded as they left the trees, their horses slowing slightly as the ground became rockier. "I suppose being the duke, or the duke's son when I was younger, has by definition made me a little…aloof."

Hattie swallowed the retort she would have given to the man if she had met him only yesterday. It would not have been far off the criticism she had leveled at him before she had known to whom she was speaking.

"The master is almost never at home, and when he is, he hardly bothers to talk to his neighbors. And so we don't bother much with him."

The words had been true and she would not take them back. And yet, now that she was starting to know the man better, they also felt hollow.

This wasn't a man who purposefully ostracized himself from the world. He had slipped into those habits accidentally, never quite knowing how, never able to extricate himself.

"Aloof is probably the right word," Hattie said eventually.

Joseph chuckled darkly. "You were going to say something far more cutting."

"No I wasn't!" she said defensively.

"Yes, you were, and you would probably be within your right to do so," he said with a shake of his head. "You know, I liked you more when you spoke more openly, Hattie. When you told me your mind directly without any fear of me. Is it knowing I am a duke? Or perhaps the fact that I am paying you now?"

Hattie jutted out her chin, glaring furiously before the immediate ire disappeared. "Perhaps both," she admitted. "But if you want, I can be direct and blunt with my honesty?"

And then she realized what she was doing. Was she…flirting with the Duke of Wincham?

"I'd appreciate that." He grinned.

Hattie smiled weakly. Well, she had asked for it. "I think you probably are aloof because of your title and your upbringing. But you choose to remain that way."

Already she knew she had gone too far.

Joseph's—the Duke of Wincham's—eyebrows had both raised. "Is that so?"

Hattie took a deep breath. "I think you could choose to spend more time with your neighbors, or the villagers. I think you could spend more time in town and see your friends, or invite them here. You've got the room!"

"That I certainly have," said Joseph dryly.

"But you choose not to," persisted Hattie, hating the way he just looked at her with that sardonic grin. "You like being alone. You like being distant. You like feeling superior to everyone around you, but if you truly knew other people, you might have to admit…well. That they are in some ways more superior than you."

There. The words were spoken. Words Hattie could not take back even if she tried.

For what felt like an eternity but was probably only a minute, they rode in silence. The chilly air only grew colder. Hattie's stomach had tied itself into a knot so tight it would probably never come undone.

And then Joseph spoke. "You really think that?"

Hattie sighed. "Yes. No. Most of the time. I am sorry, I shouldn't have—"

"No, don't apologize," he said softly without looking at her. "It's…refreshing. Oddly refreshing, actually, to hear someone speak of me in that way."

Hattie couldn't have felt more wretched if he'd tried. Perhaps he had. "I meant—"

"I know what you meant," Joseph said, and this time, he did look around. There was a hint of a smile dancing on his lips. "And though I do not think it excuses my behavior, I think there are parts of my childhood that may…well. Explain it, perhaps."

Though her instinct was to ask questions, to demand he tell all, Hattie managed to fight those reflexes. Something told her this wasn't a story one could force out of another. It had to come gradually.

Joseph sighed heavily. "Being an only child of a duke…it isn't something I would wish on anyone."

"What, all that money such a burden?" Hattie said before she could stop herself.

She actually let go of her reins to place both hands over her mouth, horrified at what she had just said. What had she been thinking?

"What do you mean by that?" came the expected defensive reply.

She swallowed. "I just…you must know that your steward pushes your tenants beyond what they can bear! Last winter, the Browns had a difficult harvest and Reverend McKee wrote to you, requesting on their behalf that their rent could be delayed."

Joseph was staring. "He did?"

"And your steward, he said—"

"My steward?" he repeated.

Hattie could barely think what to say next, but it appeared

she did not need to speak. The words kept spilling from her. "You could have been kind, but—"

"Hattie, I never saw this letter," Joseph said slowly. "My steward…he must have forgotten…"

Well, she could kiss goodbye the fifty pounds a month she had been earning, Hattie thought as heat boiled in her cheeks. Her reputation would be ruined; no one would ever want to work with her again now that the Duke of Wincham would be disposing of her services. That meant she was going to lose the farm, everything she'd worked for, her home—

"Hattie, can you hear me?"

Hattie blinked. Bramble had come to a stop alongside Maximus. Joseph was looking concerned.

Hattie tried to smile, but her shame was too heavy. "Joseph, I should never have—"

"Think nothing of it," he said softly.

He was a martyr. "Why?"

"Because you just called me Joseph," the duke said with a teasing laugh. "Dear God, so that's what did it. I like hearing you call me Joseph."

Hattie had not believed her cheeks could be any pinker, but if the sensation was anything to go by, they definitely were.

What was happening here? Was she really riding the hill trail with a duke who wanted to be called Joseph? Who laughed when she offended him, grinned when she teased him, and argued with her orders but eventually obeyed them?

"Please," Hattie said faintly, picking up her reins and nudging her mare forward. "You were telling me. About being an only child."

"It's not a unique tale, I am sure," Joseph said with a shrug. "My parents expected the best, expected me to be the best. Nothing I achieved at school or university, however, could ever compare to the name I was born to. The reputation I had to uphold. The tradition that was mine to safekeep."

Hattie couldn't help but feel a bit sorry for him. As they

neared the top of the hill, her favorite part of the trail, she tried to imagine what it was like to bear such a burden of responsibility.

"It sounds lonely," she said quietly.

"It was. It is, I suppose," said Joseph as they rounded a corner and looked out onto the spectacular view. "And yet I go on alone. Perhaps I do keep people away, Hattie, but I find…I find I do not know precisely how to draw them close."

Shivers rushed down her spine as they pulled their steeds to a halt.

She had never heard any man speak so openly. The thought that a duke could feel that way, a duke with piles of money and a large home and all the comforts a person could be afforded…

It was not something she had considered.

"What an incredible view," Hattie breathed with a sigh. "Every time I come up here, I forget how beautiful it is."

"Very beautiful," Joseph said slowly, turning to look at her. "Very beautiful indeed."

Hattie's heart skipped a beat.

Which was ridiculous, she told herself. *He didn't mean you! Look at that view; look at the way the horizon tilts along the beautiful fields! Look at the woodland, the church down there, everything looks like a painting! That was what he meant, Hattie Godwin. Not you.*

"Thank you," he said softly.

Hattie's head jerked up. "What did you say?"

"Thank you," Joseph said again. "I know it probably sounds strange; I don't think I thank you enough."

"I don't imagine you thank most people enough," Hattie said without thinking.

This time, her cheeks did not pink too badly as Joseph's laughed echoed around the hilltop.

"I suppose not," he said ruefully. "But then, no one has earned it like you."

Chapter Nine

December 15, 1810

JOSEPH SHOULD HAVE known he would be disappointed even before he opened his eyes.

He knew that sound. If he had been even more awake, he would have realized what it meant. But he had not slept this well in…what? Weeks? Months?

Doctor Walsingham had told him countless times that sleep would return. That over time, his mind would let go of the cares of the day and permit him to drift into a slumber that would be truly restful.

Joseph had yet to experience it. His increasing ire at the promises unfulfilled had doubtless made it even more difficult to fall asleep, so he had spent the last few months constantly exhausted, his mind crying out for true rest.

Until tonight.

He stirred, warm under the covers, delighting in that strange feeling one has when slowly rising from deep sleep into wakefulness.

Joseph could not recall the last time he had been this comfortable. He smiled, eyes still shut, as the gentle pattering against his windows drummed a calm rhythm.

Then his eyes snapped open.

Pattering against his windows?

"Oh, hell," he muttered, glancing at the thick green curtains.

He didn't need to draw them to know what the noise was. He should have expected it, really. They had been due heavy rain for a few days. That's what his steward had said, and the man seemed to know the weather and the land better than anyone.

And Joseph supposed, in a way, he was glad. The more rain in the dark winter months the better, he had always thought. Let the clouds get it out of their system now to give them a beautiful sunny summer.

But not now.

Heart twisting with irritation, Joseph struggled to kick back his bedcovers. "Damnit!"

It had always been so much easier with two legs of equal length.

By the time he had managed to disentangle himself, the rain had increased its pace. By the time he had reached the window, hopping as he refused to pick up his crutch for such a short distance, Joseph pulled back the curtains.

His gaze fell despondently on what would have been a view of the south gardens. As it was, the rain was so thick and heavy, all he could see was a blur.

Joseph's shoulders slumped. "Damn and blast it. Heaven forbid I get a dry day today!"

Why it mattered so much, he could not precisely tell. At least, Joseph would not admit it to anyone who asked. No one was foolish enough to ask why the master was in such high dudgeon.

It was all he could do not to snap at the footmen as they served him breakfast.

"Go on, clatter those dishes some more!" was all Joseph permitted himself to say when a footman allowed a platter's lid to fall just an inch.

The footman had colored and Joseph hated himself for saying it, but there was no way to take back the words now. They were said.

It left him, if possible, in an even worse mood. And he knew why.

"Tomorrow then. Tomorrow we'll meet at your stables at eleven o'clock and go for another long ride—I have an idea of a trail that will take into account different terrain, useful for you to practice your balance..."

Joseph clenched his fists as he walked, crutch tightly pulled into his side, along the Long Gallery. Hattie's words from yesterday echoed in his mind. The rain continued to batter against the windows. Taunting him.

It had been too good to be true, hadn't it? There he had been, genuinely excited to go on another ride with Hattie—with Miss Godwin. That was probably how he should think of her, even if he had finally managed to convince her to call him Joseph, which was rebellious in itself.

And he had to wake up to this, Joseph thought as he glanced bad-temperedly at a window. The view was obscured from here too, the water thrashing down, the wind up.

He would have to go another whole day without seeing her. A day without Hattie.

Joseph snorted as he reached the end of the Long Gallery and turned around, stretching out his stride unconsciously.

It was all foolish, he knew. Why, a month ago he had never bothered to meet the Godwins' daughter. He wasn't even sure whether he had remembered they had a daughter.

If he had, he'd not recalled her age, or thought about her as a prospect for company.

And now...

Now, Joseph realized with a sinking feeling in his chest he was starting to find a day without her was a day entirely wasted. That if he didn't see her then he could hardly know what to do with himself.

Disappointment was pouring through him as heavily as the rain and Joseph did not know what to do with this balling energy of frustration.

How was it possible so much of his joy and delight was now intertwined with…with a horse trainer? It was shameful. It was ridiculous! It would be laughed at in town, Joseph knew, if he ever allowed his thoughts to be made public.

Not that he was ever going to share them with anyone…

And a thought flickered through his mind. It had almost slipped from his grasp, it was so slight, but Joseph latched onto it eagerly and wondered whether it would be possible.

Well, it was not as though she had forbidden him from visiting her after all? True, their interactions had all been business until now. Hattie had never invited him into her home after their lessons together, Joseph thought with a bitter rush through his heart.

Though, of course, he had not invited her into Cedarworth Lacey either.

There was a line there, Joseph knew, though precisely where it had come from or who had drawn it, he did not know.

Something keeping them apart from each other. Something ensuring they did not become too close. Whatever "too close" meant.

But why not? Why not send a footman over with a note, inviting her here—or, Joseph thought with a lurch in his stomach, why not call his carriage and visit her? It was not as though she would be entertaining anyone else…would she?

And a rush of jealousy as he had never felt before burned across Joseph's skin. The mere thought of Hattie entertaining another, of talking with them, listening to their tales, perhaps even laughing at their jests…

Joseph's hand tightened on his crutch again, skin turning white at the tension.

She owed him nothing. Yet he felt a—a deep sense of ownership over her. Of possession. Of needing her.

He straightened up, finding himself halfway down the Long Gallery and not actually moving. When had he stopped walking?

Well, that didn't matter. He needed to call a footman—

"Your Grace."

Joseph jumped. It was perhaps credit to Hattie's lessons over the last few weeks that he did not subsequently tip over—not that he was grateful for that at the moment.

"Blast it all, Coulter, what do you think you're doing, creeping up on me?"

The butler bowed. "I do apologize, Your Grace. I did knock, you see."

Joseph glared over at the door his servant was pointing at, as though that could corroborate his story.

He turned back to the butler. "What do you want?"

Coulter bowed once more. "Merely to bring you this morning's post, Your Grace."

He held out three letters.

Joseph glared. Finding he could not actually take offense at his servant completing one of his tasks, he snatched the letters ill-temperedly from the man and gave him a nod.

The butler did not need any further instruction. Bowing low, Coulter stepped out of the Long Gallery and closed the door behind him with a snap.

When Joseph was absolutely certain the man had departed, he stomped over to a window and leaned against the sill with a sigh.

Blast. It was still raining. For a moment there, he hadn't paid attention to the constant thrumming of the pouring precipitation.

Looking at the three letters in his hand, Joseph leaned his crutch against the wall and moved the papers around to see the handwriting.

One was evidently a bill. He did not need to know who sent it; that was a lawyer's hand and there could only be one reason a lawyer would write to him. He wanted money for something or other, and that meant the letter could be read and dealt with by his new steward.

The second appeared to have been written by a very fine

hand. A lady's hand, if he was any judge.

A flicker of excitement sparked through Joseph's hand. Was it possible—had Hattie been thinking the same as him? Had she been similarly disappointed they were unable to ride together today?

Had she, in fact, taken the initiative ahead of him—he would not be surprised—and written to invite him to visit?

Joseph almost ripped the letter in half in his haste to open it, but the moment his gaze flashed to the end of the letter, desperate to see the way she wrote her name, a sinking feeling fell heavy through his chest.

From your faithful yet irritated great-aunt
Lady Romeril

Joseph sighed. What on earth could Lady Romeril be doing writing to him? Did she not know he had asked all London correspondence to be sent to the Dulverton Club? There it could be properly handled by one of the footmen there: carefully alphabetized, placed in his pigeon hole for up to four and twenty days, then unceremoniously burned.

It was the only way Joseph knew how to deal with such volume of letters.

Obviously his great-aunt had managed to discover this, Joseph thought grimly. There could be no other reason for sending a letter here.

He cast his eye over the long letter, phrases and sentences jumping out as he read.

Mysterious absence from town is absolutely ridiculous...

I have told them many times it will only be a matter of time before you return. Would you wish to make a liar of me, my boy?

...card party simply is nothing without you there, and I will have you know I have lost almost three guineas, and it is all your fault!

Joseph smiled despite himself. There was no one quite like Lady Romeril—he had never been permitted to call her Great-Aunt Romeril, or God forbid, Great-Aunt Arabella. Most of his childhood, he had been under the impression she was his aunt. She had been excellent at lying about her age.

That left the final letter.

His gaze drifted over to it as his heart sank lower. That had not been written by a lady, and so his hopes that Hattie had been likewise eager to see him were dashed.

It was with not much joy, therefore, that he opened the third letter.

To Your Grace, Joseph Chisholm,

I hope this letter finds you well. The entire regiment sends its regards and we all hope that your injury, though serious, is healing well.

We had hoped to see you back in France by Christmas, but it appears your unfortunate absence will continue. A shame, we could have done with your services. There is much here to be thankful for, I suppose...

Joseph jerked his gaze away from the lines and looked once more at the pouring rain. Somehow, that did not seem so bad.

A letter from one of his old friends, another spy in France. It should have lifted his spirits. It should have pleased him to know he was so sorely missed.

All it did was pool guilt into his stomach.

He should be there. That was what he had promised himself. That as he could do nothing for the war effort here at home, or in London, he would go over to France and use whatever charm he had and the plentiful titles he possessed to get his way into the Frenchies' plans.

And it had worked for months. Until...

Joseph swallowed, pushing aside the remembrances of a difficult and painful time. He was not going to think about it. Not at all.

It was a painful reminder, the letter in his hand, that he had not done as he had originally intended. He had not gone back to France.

He crumpled the letter up and placed it on the windowsill. He'd have to burn it later; he couldn't risk a servant finding it. Discovering how he was greatly missed back in France but had not gone. The last thing he wanted was for Hattie—

"There you are," said a pleasant, familiar voice behind him. "And here I was, thinking you'd be in the stables."

Joseph whirled around.

It was testament to his practice that he did not fall at the sudden movement. He could not help but twist rapidly, though. Not at the sound of that voice.

Hattie Godwin was standing in the doorway, hands on her hips, her breeches and boots splattered with mud and a fleck of it on her cheek. She was also smiling.

"S-Stables?" Joseph stammered.

How he hated the weakness in his voice! But he had been so startled to see her. This was his home. Hattie had only been inside once and that had not exactly gone according to plan…

"What the devil are you doing here?"

"I suppose I could ask you the same thing. Still leeching off your friend Wincham's good graces, I suppose?"

Joseph winced. Well, he would simply have to do better this time, that was all. This was a chance, perhaps, to impress. To show her what a duke—

"Are you just going to stand there and gawp?" asked Hattie lightly, stepping into the Long Gallery and allowing the door to close behind her. "Goodness, what a marvelous gallery."

Joseph swallowed. He needed to get ahold of himself! He needed to say something, preferably with a little sense and a great deal of mirth. Now, what could he say…?

"Long Gallery," he said with an idiotic grin.

Long Gallery? Long Gallery! What on earth was wrong with—?

"So I see," said Hattie, turning this way and that, looking up the length of the place. "I suppose this is where you've been practicing then?"

Joseph nodded, swallowing all his nerves and hoping to goodness no one else would ever see him in such a state.

How did she do it? She was no lady, merely a commoner, yet she had the effect on him that a royal princess would. Absolutely tongue tied. Like a fool!

"I spoke to my steward," he blurted out.

Hattie blinked. "You…you did?"

Joseph fought the instinct to twist his fingers together. "He never told me that the…goodness, I can't remember their names—"

"The Browns," she said faintly.

He nodded. "If I had known they were in difficulties—I am not a harsh master, nor landlord. Not if I knew—my steward has left my employ."

Why did he wish her to be impressed? It had not been done merely to please her. Joseph knew he needed a steward he could trust, and if letters intended for him had not arrived to his hand, that could not continue.

Still. It was another benefit to see her eyes widen.

"Oh," she said quietly.

Joseph nodded again, feeling foolish. "I thought you should know."

"I can't believe you actually listened to me," she said with a short laugh. "I…well, I am unaccustomed to gentlemen paying heed to a woman's words."

There was such bitterness in her voice, Joseph found himself leaning forward. Who had hurt this woman? Her father?

"Well, as pleasant as this most certainly is," Hattie said, striding toward him and standing by him at the window. "I rather thought you would want to go for a ride."

Joseph's jaw fell open, all his panic disappearing. "Are you moon-touched, woman? It's pouring with rain!"

"Is it?" asked Hattie innocently.

Joseph stared. Then he jerked his head to the window.

Well. It had been raining. It was certainly still spitting from what he could see. It wasn't dry, that he could say with absolute certainty.

"It's wet," he said foolishly.

Joseph's stomach cringed as he heard his own words. How was this happening? He had never been one to admire the beauty and elegance of ladies. At least, he noticed it. He just did not permit himself to be awed by it.

Until now. Until he stood beside Hattie Godwin and breathed her in. Until his gaze flickered over the thin white shirt she was wearing, tucked into her breeches and accentuating her waist. Until he saw the fleck of mud on her cheek and longed to reach up a hand and—

"Wh-What are you doing?" Hattie said quietly, eyes widening.

"It's just—you've got a bit of—there," said Joseph softly.

His hand had risen despite himself. His fingers brushed the soft cheek of the woman who was fast becoming the only reason he wished to rise from bed every morning.

Which was ridiculous. She certainly saw him as nothing but…but a man, Joseph knew. A man who needed fixing. She saw him as a project, a client, that was all.

"Oh," said Hattie, her cheeks flushing as she raised a hand to where his fingers had been but a moment ago. "Thank you."

Joseph's breath caught in his throat. They were so close. He'd barely noticed it, so intoxicated he had been by her mere presence.

But now he did think about it; she was but a few inches from him. She had placed herself there; she had wanted to be close to him. And why would she do that? Surely because—

"Are we going on that ride?" Hattie said, stepping away and toward the door.

Joseph quickly righted himself, hoping to goodness she had not noticed his sudden lunge. "Ride?"

"It's not raining. Well, hardly," said Hattie with a grin. "And a duke should be ready for anything!"

Joseph tried to smile as his heart lurched most painfully.

No, it wasn't pain. It was something else. An ache for her.

He had always considered himself ready for anything. He was the duke. There were few things that money or prestige could not fix.

And it was only now that he realized that he was. Ready for anything, that was.

Except her.

"A ride," Joseph said stiffly, mostly to himself. "Right."

It did not take them long to leave the house and reach the stables. The stairs had, as ever, presented a slight problem, and Joseph had flushed as he struggled with the final two. *Stairs!* Stairs were his nemesis at the moment. He hoped Hattie had not noticed just how shaky his breath was by the time he reached the bottom.

As they stepped into the stable, however, his breathing had returned to normal and excitement was once again flaring in Joseph's chest.

It was not just the ride, though it was always pleasant to be out on a stallion's back. There was something…something healing about it. Joseph could not have explained it.

But it wasn't the ride on Maximus that had calmed him.

No, it was the thought of a few more hours in Hattie's company. Hours he had thought, thanks to the weather, he would be forced to forego.

And now the realization that he had her all to himself for the rest of the morning and as much of the afternoon as he could take was sparking joy throughout Joseph's chest.

"You managed that without a second thought," Hattie said approvingly as she watched him mount Maximus from the ground.

Joseph grinned, delight pouring through him. "Only thanks to your outstanding teaching."

It was unlike him to be so direct, but he saw with delight that it had quite an effect on the woman.

Hattie's cheeks blushed and her foot stumbled on the stirrup as she went to mount her mare in a stall along from Maximus. "Oh, drat!"

Joseph's heart flipped over. Was that because of him? Had he impacted her just as she had impacted him? Was it possible the kiss they had shared was not merely one, but only the beginning of—?

"Right, off we go," said Hattie briskly. "I've been considering your next lesson, and I believe we need to work on…"

Joseph's smile faded as they trotted out of the stable and into the damp misty air.

He was fooling himself. He would be a fool indeed to allow his fancy to get the better of him, and deprive him of such an excellent horse trainer merely because he misread the signs.

Hattie had been perfectly clear. And besides, Joseph had no wish to be vulnerable again. No, it was better this way. Better they keep their distance. Better he stay alone.

Chapter Ten

Hattie had been relieved when the rain had stopped. It had been the only thing keeping her from Joseph.

Keeping her from teaching the Duke of Wincham, and justifying her ridiculously large salary, she tried to tell herself. That was all. She was merely focused on being a good horse trainer. That was all.

Mostly all.

She breathed in the damp air as their horses trotted along the trail in the direction she had indicated. Hattie had considered this carefully to find the perfect route.

"Perfect?" Joseph had said when she voiced this, a lilt of teasing in his voice. "Dear God, what a pronouncement. Perfect."

And for absolutely no reason Hattie could think of, her cheeks flushed with heat as he spoke and looked at her.

She was getting ahead of herself. No, not ahead of herself! That was not the direction this…this partnership, for want of a better word, was going.

Hattie had always been certain on that. Not that she had ever needed to be, really. Most of the clients she'd had in the last few years had been old duffers who had bought a horse they thought looked exciting but then couldn't control.

That was the trouble with buying at auction when you didn't

know what you were looking for she had said over and over again, her throat getting sore.

Few men had listened.

There had never been any…well, attraction. Hattie could not think what else to call it. She'd never felt warm in their presence, these men old enough to be her grandfather who never bothered to trim their whiskers.

But Joseph Chisholm, Duke of Wincham…he was something different.

Hattie cast him a look as they rode toward the coast. He was holding himself differently somehow. She couldn't quite put her finger on it, and she made it her business to see how a rider sat in the saddle.

When she had first gotten the man up on Maximus, there had been an air of…the only word she could think of was defeat.

He had ridden like a man told this was a slight reprieve from his ban on horse riding and he had better not get too accustomed to it. Dejected. Shoulders slumped, eyes downcast, convinced this was the closest he would ever get to true enjoyment on a steed again.

Now look at him.

Hattie found she could not stop looking at him. Sitting tall, his collar points sharp against his jawline, which was just as cutting. His eyes flashed with pleasure, the sheer enjoyment of the ride pouring through him.

She could not help but smile. Joy, pure and unaffected, rose within her. It was always wonderful to see a client excel, of course, but this was different.

Perhaps not so pure and unaffected.

She swallowed, trying to drag her gaze back to the path. Joseph drew her attention like…like a hawk in the air.

Once you had spotted it, you could not help but stare at it, hovering perfectly in the air, unmoving in the wind. The skill, so impressive. And so though she undoubtedly had something to do, some place to be, she always found herself staring up, waiting.

Watching.

Waiting for it to swoop down and suddenly catch its prey.

Hattie's stomach lurched. Was that what she was? His prey?

"You're thinking of something important, aren't you?"

She started. "Wh-What?"

Joseph's eyes were twinkling with repressed laughter. "Nothing. Just something in the way your gaze had shifted off into the distance. What were you thinking?"

Heat colored Hattie's cheeks as she jerked her gaze back to the path. "Nothing."

Nothing, except how you dukes are surely all the same, she did not say. Seducers, taking the virtue of women left, right, and center. At least, that's what she had always thought.

She had thought dukes haughty, absent, and heartless, too. She had always presumed the mysterious and never-present Duke of Wincham to be of that nature.

But now that she was getting to know him…why, Hattie could not think of three words less suitable for the man. It was most irritating.

Knowing full well she should not be prying into the man's private affairs—more, that Joseph had made it quite clear he had little wish to speak of himself—Hattie turned to him.

"Joseph—"

"You know, I do not think I will ever tire of hearing you call me that," the duke said, cutting across her.

"If you're not careful, I will have to revert back to calling you Wincham."

"As long as you never slip back to calling me Your Grace," said Joseph with a shake of his head. "Now that, I could never endure."

Intrigue soared through Hattie's chest. *Why would he say that? Why would that be so terrible?*

Oh, she knew she would hate it. It would be most upsetting to suddenly find herself on such a cool footing with a man becoming more interesting, perhaps more dear to her, with each passing moment.

Hattie struggled with the feelings and managed to force them away.

The Duke of Wincham was her client! And if she was careful, and wise, Hattie told herself, she would do well with him—teaching him! And that would help her reputation, make it easier to keep the stud farm going. And that was all.

She slowed Bramble as they neared the cliffs, the sound of the roaring sea reaching her ears.

"I love it here."

Hattie turned to Joseph, whose face had become wistful. "Really? I thought your favorite trail was up the hill, overlooking the—"

"My favorite trail, perhaps, but this is a place I have come often all throughout my life," said Joseph quietly. "I liked to sit here and look out across the waves and think."

Hattie looked at the sea. There was something marvelous about it. Something that made one feel small and insignificant, yet at the same time, part of something huge and wonderful.

"It makes me feel small," said Joseph softly. "And yet important at the same time."

Hattie started. Her mare, not expecting the sudden movement, jerked to the left.

"Hattie, careful!"

She managed to get the horse under control in time, but that did not stop the horrendous thundering of her heart. *A few more feet to the right...*

Hattie tried to smile at Joseph, whose face was ashen. "It's fine, don't worry—"

"You could have fallen over the edge—you could have died!" Joseph's voice cracked. "Don't ever do that to me again, Hattie! Do you hear me?"

Hattie swallowed. There was such power in his demand, but also such brokenness. Such vulnerability.

Though it had been her and her horse which had almost

slipped over the edge of the cliff, falling to oblivion, it was Joseph who looked the most shaken.

And despite herself, Hattie's attention was drawn once more to the knot of his breeches just before his left knee.

How had it happened? Had there been a terrible accident? Had he perhaps fallen?

"I'm fine," Hattie said, trying to reassure him.

But Joseph had tugged his reins and moved Maximus at least six feet further inland. "Come on. Please, I-I don't want you too close to the edge. You're too precious, Hattie."

The moment she met his gaze, Hattie knew the words had slipped from his tongue without his prior planning. There was a look of horror mingled with passion on Joseph's face, and she knew she could only do one thing in response.

Murmuring quietly to her mare, she brought her alongside Maximus, now about ten feet from the edge of the cliff.

"How about we go a little further inland," Hattie said quietly, hardly able to meet his eyes. "I think the sun will soon be out."

It was a foolish thing to say, but in that moment, she had just needed to say something. Anything to distract from the fact the Duke of Wincham had just called her precious.

Joseph glanced upward. "Sun, you say?"

Hattie had opened her mouth to respond, but a rain drop fell on her nose, halting her speech in her tracks.

The sun had all but disappeared behind the dark cloud which had somehow rolled over the horizon without her noticing. Her attention had been far too taken up with the handsome man riding beside her, visibly concerned for her safety.

As he would have been for anyone, Hattie told herself firmly. What sort of monster would have been happy with the thought of a woman falling over a cliff? It was nothing more than that. She was going to get herself twisted into all sorts of knots if she did not remember.

"The sun will return," Hattie said bracingly, nudging her mare into a trot. "Any moment now."

They rode in silence for several minutes, Hattie determinedly ignoring the rain drops falling more frequently now.

Only when she caught Joseph's eyes, his face full of mirth and his lips pursed together to prevent laughter, did she finally relent.

"Fine!" Hattie said with a dry laugh. "It's raining!"

"Hattie Godwin, it is absolutely pouring!" said Joseph with a chuckle, shaking his head. "Why on earth did you think this was a good idea again?"

Hattie shrugged as rain scattered down, turning his blue coat a dark navy and her father's old green coat a much darker mossy color. "It felt like a good idea at the time—it wasn't raining then!"

Joseph laughed again and the warmth in it fired up warmth in her chest.

Another man may have complained. He may have blamed her, though Hattie hardly knew how it was her fault. Other than the fact that she had suggested the ride that was. Still. She hardly controlled the weather!

Joseph's hair was rapidly dampening, drips starting to slip from his collar. Hattie was sure she must look similarly bedraggled, and wished she could look like…

Well. The ladies she had seen on the few rare occasions her parents attended a gathering in the village. The ladies with the beautiful silk gowns, feathers in their hair, jewelry glittering in candlelight.

Poised and perfect, and certainly not drenched in the rain like a drowned rat.

Hattie leaned back in her saddle, and tried not to think about it.

"I'll race you."

Her head snapped to the side. "I beg your pardon?"

She must have misheard the man—though Joseph did have a mischievous, almost wicked grin. She had never seen him look so…so cheerful.

"I'll race you," said Joseph. "Over there, to the edge of that field. First one there—"

"Last one there's a rotten egg!" Hattie cried, digging her heels into Bramble's side.

Her horse reacted quickly, as she had known she would. Going from a trot to a gallop almost in a heartbeat, Hattie's pulse thundered as they roared forward together.

There was no sight of Joseph—*and there wouldn't be,* Hattie thought, heart sinking. Why, they had not progressed to a canter with Maximus yet. There was no possibility he—

"Try to keep up, Hattie!" bellowed Joseph with a laugh as he pulled up alongside her.

Hattie could not help it. She laughed with him. The rain was pouring, thicker than ever, and mud flew up around them as their horses thundered across the field. This was—this was glorious!

There was nothing else like it. Nothing like racing forward as fast as you could, wind whipping through your hair, raindrops cascading down, with a man by your side who was enjoying the spectacle just as much as you.

And Hattie knew in that moment she could do this forever. Not ride in the rain, per se, but be with him. Joseph. There was something about him that challenged her, true, but there was more to him than that.

He wasn't just a man without two legs. He wasn't even just a duke.

Joseph was someone who constantly surprised her, constantly made her feel more alive than she ever had before.

As they reached the edge of the field, racing toward them far swifter than she had expected, she knew precisely what she was going to do.

"Aha!" said Joseph triumphantly, his horse a mere nose ahead. "I win—Hattie!"

Hattie reveled in this moment. Leaning forward, urging on her mare with everything within her, she soared through the air.

For a moment, she was flying.

Oh, this was living. This was what her father had always forbidden, the one part of riding he had said was unsuitable for a lady, much less his daughter.

And Hattie had not done it since—since he had died.

But in this moment, it was the perfect thing to do. Hanging in the air as though time had utterly ceased, Hattie could just make out Joseph in the corner of her eye. He and Maximus were standing by the hedgerow. The duke's eyes were wide and he was watching her with amazement.

And then she and Bramble were trotting on the ground on the other side of the fence.

A roll of thunder echoed through the air as Hattie cheered loudly into the night. "Yes!"

And only then did she recollect herself.

Cheeks burning, she nudged her horse toward the hedgerow. "Ah. Yes, I would appreciate if you didn't mention—"

"Dear God, Hattie, where did you learn to ride like that?" Joseph said, awe on his face.

Hattie grinned. "How many times do I need to remind you that I run a stud farm and work as a horse trainer, Joseph?"

The man shook his head, evidently impressed. "Dear God, I thought I was going to have a heart attack when you—"

Whatever else he said, Hattie never knew. His words were lost as a flash of lightning, bright and deafening, cracked over their heads.

"The storm must be coming in right above us," Hattie said, nudging her horse along the hedgerow to the gate. "Come on, we'd better find shelter."

Hattie tried not to think of what she must look like as Joseph met her at the gate. It only took her a moment to slip from Bramble's back and open it up, but the man gained a clear look.

Her hair was soaking, shoulders drenched, and coat not much better. Her breeches were splattered with mud and there was going to be a great deal of cleaning until her boots were returned to their normal shine.

But as Hattie glanced up at Joseph as he nudged Maximus through the now open gate, she saw nothing but…well. *Desire.*

She would not have called it that aloud, of course, but it was quite clear. Hattie did not need to be particularly accustomed to the attentions of gentlemen to recognize that look. She tried not to look at the way Joseph's breeches clung to his thighs in the wet of the rain.

"There's a folly just through here. I think my grandfather built it, or someone. Dear God, I'm wet! If someone had told me I'd be doing this," Joseph said wryly as they trotted eagerly toward the cover of some trees. "I would have told them they were absolutely—"

"What, riding with a woman?" Hattie teased, before she could stop herself.

"Not quite," he said with a dry laugh.

It was perhaps the only thing dry about him. As they reached the folly, a small sort of pretend Roman temple, Hattie saw he was completely drenched.

Well. That was not completely true. As Joseph dismounted, inelegantly but on his own, Hattie saw with a flush of heat to her cheeks that his buttocks were completely dry.

She should not be looking at a duke's buttocks!

"Here, do you need a hand?"

Hattie refused the offer, slipping from her mare with very little difficulty. "You go into the folly."

Joseph obeyed immediately, which was odd in itself. She did not follow. "Hattie?"

Hattie called over her shoulder. "I'll be there in a minute!"

Her fingers were busy ensuring the reins of both horses were tied securely to a large branch of an oak tree. Though her hands and the leather were soaked, she managed it.

"What were you doing?" Joseph asked as she scampered into the folly, dripping on the marble floor.

Hattie pushed hair from her eyes and blinked up at the tall man. "What do you mean?"

"With the horses," he pointed.

She glanced over her shoulder to ensure the two horses were

still there. "Tying them up. Horses are not known for their love of thunder and lightning, and if they bolted—well, we're still only half a mile from the cliff."

"But you're even more soaked!"

Hattie looked back steadily. "I wouldn't let anything happen to those horses."

For a moment, she thought the duke was going to argue with her.

Then Joseph's face softened. "You take good care of them, don't you?"

There was such tenderness in his tone, Hattie hardly knew where to look. "They're easier than people."

The admission was a strange one. Not that she wouldn't say as much to anyone that asked. It was the truth, and she stood by it.

No, it was the situation itself. There they stood, merely a foot from each other, in a Roman temple with rain drumming on the roof. Water dripped, cascaded, poured down the columns around the edge, and there was another roll of thunder as she spoke.

And Hattie was with Joseph. The two of them alone, in this weather.

"You…you're taking good care of me, you know."

Heat swelled in Hattie's chest.

No, it wasn't heat—it was desire. Perhaps it was both. Something in her knew this was her chance to voice what she had been unable to say the last time they had been this close. Not just physically. Their intimacy was something far different.

"I—I didn't expect—"

"I am sorry. My mistake. It won't happen again."

The boldness Hattie had always forced down, been told was unladylike and most unbecoming, rose again.

And this time, she didn't fight it. "I would do more than that if…if you'd let me."

For a moment, she wasn't sure whether he had understood her. She had been quite indirect, after all, and—

"Oh, Hattie," Joseph breathed before pulling her into his arms.

She went willingly. This was what she wanted, what she had craved the moment the duke had kissed her before. This closeness, this pleasure, this sense she was the most important thing in the world.

As his lips gently parted hers and his tongue teased into her mouth, Hattie clutched him. The wetness of their clothes somehow heightened the pleasure she felt, somehow bringing them closer than she could have possibly imagined.

"What in God's name—?"

"Ah," Hattie said helplessly. Joseph was staring at—"I always keep a knife on me, it's safest that way."

Joseph raised an eyebrow. "You have nothing to fear from me."

"I know," she said quickly, heart still thundering. "But sometimes…"

No. She would not tell him. Joseph did not need to know about Edward. No one did.

"It's useful for working with horses to have a knife on you," Hattie said instead, wishing to goodness that she was back in his arms. "Joseph…"

His eyes darkened as he heard her voice, heard the need. He pulled her back into his embrace.

Hattie whimpered, unable to help herself. This was wonderful, his kisses sparking a fire in her she could not understand and did not wish to.

And his hands were moving, moving in ways Hattie could never have expected. With every inch of her body heightened, anticipation curled around her heart as Joseph's hands moved slowly from her waist to her hips, to her buttocks…

"Dear God, I've got to stop," said Joseph, panting as he released her and leaned back.

The sudden absence of him was as bad as a wound. Hattie could not understand it. The world had made sense when she was in his arms. Now that she wasn't anymore, it was all wrong.

Lightning flashed above them.

"You don't have to stop," Hattie breathed.

Joseph's eyes widened as though he could not believe what he had heard. "You…you want me to keep going?"

"I want you—I need you to keep kissing me," said Hattie, the words spilling out of her and all thought of embarrassment forgotten. "Please, Joseph."

And she was once more in his arms, her back pressed up against a column as Joseph poured kisses down onto her lips more frantically than the heavens poured the rain.

Chapter Eleven

December 19, 1810

"WELL," SAID JOSEPH awkwardly, not sure what to say. "What…should we do now?"

His heart curled at the ungainliness of his question, but he could think of no other way to ask it as both he and Hattie entered the cavernous hallway of his home.

It had been her suggestion in the first place. After their ride that afternoon, which had been a joy, they had trotted their horses back into the stables, into the waiting arms of Knowles.

"I'll get them rubbed down after all that exercise," the stablehand had said. "Including your mare, Miss Hattie, if that is suitable."

Joseph had been forced to hide a smile. It said a great deal that Knowles had made the offer; he had seen the slight awkwardness between the two of them, and could only assume it was some sort of professional rivalry they had managed to keep out of sight.

Hattie's stiff but friendly, "Thank you, Mr. Knowles," had confirmed it.

And as the stablehand had taken the horses inside, he and Hattie had stood outside the stable in obstinate silence.

Joseph had not known precisely what to say. What words to say had been a constant problem since their passionate kissing the folly just five days before.

"You...you want me to keep going?"

"I want you—I need you to keep kissing me. Please, Joseph."

They had agreed, once they had managed to keep their hands off each other, not to speak of the situation again. It was surely something to do with all the lightning in the sky, Joseph had muttered. Hattie had mumbled something about heightened feelings after the ride.

Joseph privately thought her near death experience was surely top of her mind as she had clung to him.

So they had not spoken of it. Not two days ago, when they had met for a short ride, the terrible weather forbidding anything else. And not today, when they had gone along the long forest path, the trees mostly silent as birds nested for the winter and animals hibernated.

Yet it hovered, didn't it? Above them, around them, Joseph could hardly move for thinking about those kisses. The way she had melted into his arms. Had clung to him.

The sensation of her between him and the column...

Into that silence,

Hattie said suddenly, "Why haven't you invited me into your home, Joseph?"

Joseph had smiled at that, though with a certain element of discomfort. Not purely because a pair of stable lads had passed by at that moment, eyes agog that anyone would consider calling the master by his first name.

Because it was a question he had been asking himself the entire walk. How could he elongate his time with Miss Hattie Godwin?

She had other responsibilities, probably. Only now that they had walked across the stables, around the house, and through the large front doors into the hallway did Joseph realize Hattie's existence was probably not orbiting around him.

Why, she had mentioned a stud farm before, hadn't she? Why had he never realized that she was breeding horses up there? Still, he had hoped for an excuse to spend another hour with her, maybe two, and she had now given him that.

Which did not explain why they were now standing in the hallway in silence.

"Well. What...what do you want to do now?"

His inelegant words echoed around the large hall. Joseph had never noticed how big it was before. Now that he saw it through Hattie's eyes, it was ridiculous.

Hattie tilted her head back to take in the huge ceiling. "My goodness."

"It's all rather ostentatious," said Joseph hastily. "Not my style at all."

She raised an eyebrow. "Really? What is your style?"

Joseph opened his mouth, realized he had absolutely no idea what he was about to say, then closed it.

What was his style?

It was an interesting question, one he had never considered. After all, he was a duke. There was only one style: that which one inherited.

There had been generations of Winchams living in these walls, each one of them adding something to the décor. His mother had completely redecorated the morning room, and the study was all his father. The library was his grandfather's design, apparently, and his great-grandfather was responsible for the Long Gallery.

No one had currently admitted fault for the way the billiards room was laid out, but there it was.

Everyone had contributed something to the Cedarworth Lacey...except him.

"Joseph?"

Joseph blinked. Hattie was waving a hand before his eyes.

"You'd completely gone there," she said cheerfully. "What were you thinking?"

Joseph hesitated. He had never known anyone for being so…so direct with their questions. No one ever asked him what he was thinking. They just waited for his orders.

"Ah, Your Grace and…guest," came the smooth tones of his butler.

Joseph turned to Coulter with some relief. "There you are. Be so good as to take Hattie—take Miss Godwin's coat."

If only Hattie didn't have to flush so violently! Joseph was almost certain he would have kept his composure if her cheeks had not pinked so delightfully.

As it was, his stomach lurched. Dear God, he was in danger. Very real danger. This wasn't just a kiss with a woman after a dance while her father wasn't looking. This was—

"Very good, Your Grace," said Coulter calmly. "The drawing room has a fire lit—"

"We'll be in the library, I think," Joseph said suddenly, gripping his crutch tightly. *This could be a mistake, but…* "Ensure there's a fire lit, will you?"

His butler met his gaze. There was curiosity there Joseph had never seen before.

Well, he very rarely did anything out of the ordinary. His servants knew his routine like clockwork, and there was so little variation, they merely followed the tedium of every day.

But this was different.

"Very good, Your Grace," the servant repeated. "The library. I shall take care of it."

Joseph turned to start walking as his butler slipped into the servants' corridor. Only then did he realize that Hattie was not with him. "Hattie?"

"My goodness," she said in a mock whisper, moving to his side and giggling. "I forget sometimes that you're a duke. Then here you are, issuing orders, having them obeyed—"

"Something you could learn from," Joseph said with an attempt at teasing.

He was not sure whether he had spoken out of turn—but

Hattie grinned. "You know, obeying orders is not something I am particularly proficient at."

"So I have seen," Joseph said dryly as they stepped along the West Corridor.

It was a corridor he had known since he was a child. He'd learn to toddle along here, and had been told off numerous times for running along it. Not that he'd ever run along it again, Joseph could not help but think wryly.

"My word, some of these paintings are rather grand," she breathed, gaze darting over them. "Is that a Gainsborough?"

"One of five we have, I think," Joseph said rather awkwardly.

Only now did he realize just how closed his circle of acquaintances truly was.

After all, there was Penshaw, Caelfall, even Martock at times, when he wasn't being a complete beast. He'd known Axwick almost as long as he could remember. Chantmarle was almost a part of the family…

It was as he thought this that Joseph realized, with a lurch to his stomach, that they were all…dukes.

Had he ever walked down the West Corridor with someone who wasn't from a lineage like his own? Had he ever, Joseph thought with a jolt, walked with a woman?

"So beautiful," Hattie mused, her fingers trailing along a gold gilt frame.

Joseph nodded. How had he never noticed it before? The painting truly was beautiful. A landscape scene, a pair of horses galloping across it. You could see the wind in their manes.

"Yes," he said aloud, gaze slipping once more to the woman who was fast becoming his sole definition of beautiful. "Yes, beautiful."

Hattie caught his gaze and swiftly dropped her hand. "Where is this library of yours then?"

Joseph pointed. "Third door along, on the left."

When they stepped into the room, he saw Coulter had moved more quickly than he had thought possible. Small flames were flickering in the grate, a fire newly lit. It was already filling the room with warmth.

Joseph gestured toward an armchair by the fire. "Please."

Hattie bobbed what would have been a curtsey if she had been wearing a gown then curled up in the chair like a cat.

He almost commented on it. He had never seen anyone sit like that. He had been raised, after all, to hold himself stiff and proud. It was most uncomfortable, now that he came to think of it. But that was how a duke sat.

But Hattie? She was fluid, loose. She curled up into a position that looked remarkably comfortable. Perhaps when alone, he would have to try it.

"Please," Hattie said with a grin, gesturing to the chair opposite.

Joseph chuckled under his breath as he obeyed her direction, allowing his crutch to fall to the ground as he sank into the welcoming arm chair. "You know, I don't think anyone has ever invited me to sit in my own home before."

"That is because you do not have enough guests over," Hattie pointed out as the fire crackled. "I am sure there is a lady in your acquaintance who wishes to be so bold. If only to attract your attention."

Joseph's ears pricked up. *Now, was there a hint of jealousy in her voice?*

Perhaps he was imagining it. Perhaps he was hoping for it. But did Hattie look pink?

"If I had people here, which I never do as you know, I would fain expect a lady to be so bold and outrageous," Joseph said, hoping she understood his merriment to be a tease.

It appeared she did. Hattie placed a hand on her heart as though outraged by his comment. "Why, I do declare, I have never been so insulted!"

"I suppose not," said Joseph, flickers of excitement rushing through his bones. "I would venture to hope I will only ever be the man to insult you."

His memory soared back to those kisses. Hot, steamy kisses he had poured onto Hattie's lips and had been gratefully received—

Joseph examined her face. Was she not willing to meet his eye, or was that a trick of the dying afternoon light?

"I can't think what you mean," Hattie said quietly.

Discomfort swelled in Joseph's chest. Oh hell, how had he managed to lose the light and vibrant air they had so recently enjoyed?

There couldn't actually be a gentleman in her past, could there?

Joseph racked his brains to try and remember whether Hattie had ever mentioned a gentleman's name to him. He could not think of one. Oh, she had talked of Mr. Knowles, but there was no love lost there.

So why on earth—

"So, you can now ride," Hattie said firmly, changing the conversation. "You can mount from the ground, canter—"

"Almost gallop," Joseph interjected, rather proud of the speeds he and Maximus had managed that afternoon before they had lost the brightness of the day. "At rather impressive speeds, if I say so myself."

Hattie's eyes twinkled, and the joy of their conversation returned. "I'm not sure I would call it impressive—"

"How very dare you!"

"My point was about to be, what do you want to do now?"

Joseph swallowed. What he wanted, very much, was to move Hattie to the sofa just to his right, join her, and then kiss—

"With riding, I meant," Hattie said, a knowing look in her eye. "Don't you be thinking of that, Joseph Chisholm."

She was far too knowledgeable for her own good, Joseph thought darkly. There's a woman who would be difficult to convince into something she didn't want to do. More's the pity. He was almost certain he could tempt her into—

"Joseph!"

"Yes, yes, fine, riding," said Joseph hastily, though he grinned at her scandalized look. And she didn't technically know what he had been thinking. "I think I would like to…to hunt."

Well. It was not a complete lie.

Most of the skills one would need for hunting were precisely the same as what he would need for when he returned to France. And he would be hunting there, of a sort. Hunting down French information.

It was essentially the same. He wasn't *lying*.

"Hunting?" asked Hattie with a raised eyebrow. "I did not know you hunted much. I've never been invited to a hunt anyway."

Guilt seared through Joseph's chest. Of course she hadn't. Miss Godwin was not a lady; she had no title, no father of note. As far as he was aware, she had no fortune, and she had never mingled in his circles so she had no connections. There would have been no cause to invite such a woman.

By God, to think he could have met her years ago. Spent years in her company—

"What an oversight," Joseph said aloud in an attempt to stop thinking.

Hattie did not appear convinced. "Not impressive enough for your guest list was I."

It was not a question. "Sadly not," Joseph said weakly.

How did she do it? Always say what was on his mind, or just beyond it? Say what he was too afraid to even think, yet make it something easy, increasing no discomfort and making him feel rather pleasant?

"I'm not stupid, you know."

Joseph looked up. There was a knowing sort of look on her face again, but this time Hattie's expression was tempered with kindness. Softness. Sympathy.

Joseph forced himself not to groan. Oh, no. Here it came. It always came eventually. The pity. Why did she think he had hidden himself away here?

"I know you were in the war," Hattie said softly.

Her gaze moved, as Joseph knew it would, to the absence of his left lower leg. If only he could shift it out of view, but that was impossible. The part of him that was missing would always be visible, always the first thing people looked at. Even if they could not help it. Even if they tried not to.

Joseph's jaw tightened as he said. "Not really."

"You don't have to talk about it if you don't want to," said Hattie, her voice still low and warm. "I just thought you should know…I consider you a hero. You've sacrificed so much. You're a hero."

His chest lurched painfully.

"I just thought you should know…I consider you a hero. You've sacrificed so much. You're a hero."

"I'm no hero," Joseph said forcefully. "I told you, not—I wasn't a solider."

"But you were out there, serving your country," Hattie said.

There was no force in her words. No harshness in her voice. But there was a solid sort of certainty Joseph had never met with before. This wasn't a woman he could out-argue, or press into a particular opinion. Hattie would think what she thought. That was the end of it.

Joseph dropped his head onto a hand, elbow leaning on the armchair rest. "Don't build me up to be something I'm not, Hattie. A hero? No, I don't think so. It was an accident, it was in France—"

"And you were serving your country, weren't you?"

He had promised everyone he would not speak of it. Technically, Joseph knew, he had not been a spy. He had received no formal orders, no technical training. He hadn't been told where to go or what to do. He was a duke. He was in France. He was encouraged to…familiarize himself with the locals.

It was astonishing what people would spill to a duke. Even an English one.

And he had kept his dealings there a secret from everyone.

His servants had thought him in London; his friends in London thought him a recluse at Cedarworth Lacey…and all the while, he'd been in France.

Joseph swallowed. But he had not been forbidden from telling anyone. So why was he finding it so hard to admit to Hattie?

"Fine," he said heavily. "I was in France."

"I'm proud of you."

"You don't even know me!" he shot back, a little of his old fire spilling into his words.

Joseph regretted it instantly, but Hattie did not seem cowed.

To the contrary, she held his gaze firmly. "Really? I feel like I know you. Better than most people. Perhaps…"

Her words trailed away, but Joseph knew what she had been about to say.

Perhaps better than anyone.

His stomach lurched. He wanted to talk about it. Share it with her. Somehow, knowing she felt so close to him made Joseph realize just how close they were.

Had he ever felt as comfortable with anyone as he did with Hattie Godwin?

"I had finished a…a conversation with people, in Rheims," Joseph found himself saying in a level voice.

Strange. Even just saying that, the ever-present ache in his chest seemed to lessen.

"I was riding along the road, and there was an ambush. Well, not really an ambush, more an accident." Joseph sighed. Every word lessened the pressure on his chest; he had to keep going. "French soldiers attacked, and a saber…"

No, he could not speak of that directly. Not yet. Perhaps not ever.

"Suffice to say, the wound was significant, and it was not going to get better on its own," Joseph said dryly. He caught Hattie's gaze. She was transfixed. "By the time I reached London, rot had set in. I was determined to be treated at home so I picked up Walsingham—"

"Walsingham?"

"Best doctor in London," Joseph explained. "When we reached here, the man warned me I could lose more than my leg. I could lose my life."

He shivered despite the warmth in the room.

"The leg came off," he said, deciding not to detail the rather torturous method. "And I've been here recovering ever since."

Silence fell between them. Joseph wondered whether he had been too detailed, or not enough. Hattie was looking at him with such warmth, it was only when she started to speak that he realized what was different.

It wasn't pity. It was something different. *Affection?*

"Do you think you'll ever go back?"

Joseph cleared his throat. It was not a conversation he wished to have with anyone, let alone Hattie. "Yes. No. I don't know."

Her gaze was piercing. "You feel you should go back."

"I suppose so," he admitted. "But for a long time that felt impossible. I could barely walk. The idea of returning…"

"And how does it feel now?"

Joseph's hand automatically moved to the stump. "Well, it—"

"No, I meant here," Hattie said quietly, placing her hand on her heart. "How does it feel?"

He swallowed. How had she known? "Speaking about it feels…feels better. As though a heavy anvil is lifted from my chest. As though…I can start thinking about living again."

Their eyes met and Joseph knew, without a shadow of a doubt. Oh, this wasn't the right time. He would have to think about it, consider precisely how he wished to express it.

But he was going to marry this woman.

Chapter Twelve

December 23, 1810

Hattie pushed back her curls and wished, not for the first time that afternoon, she had bothered to pin back her hair as she usually did.

That was the trouble with having such luscious, thick dark hair. Her mother said it was a trial, and now that Hattie was older, she couldn't help but agree. But as she rode so often, pinning the mane back tightly, it was pleasant every now and again to have it loose.

Even if it did keep slipping over her eyes.

Sweeping her hair over her shoulder, Hattie leaned once more over the desk.

"And if that invoice has been paid, that crosses out the final debt to the blacksmith…" Hattie muttered to herself.

She had always talked to herself when doing the accounts.

When she had been younger, she had been talking to her father. He had been insistent she understand precisely where the money was going, and where it was coming from.

"How else," he had always said, "will you know how to run this place when I'm gone?"

True, they had never expected him to be gone so quickly.

Hattie swallowed. The pain of his loss, and that of her mother's, rose suddenly and unexpectedly. It was always this way. You think you have acclimated to the lack of someone, and then all of a sudden, you haven't. You suddenly realize the huge hole they have left in your life, and wonder how you ever managed to go a single minute without thinking of them.

And the months would go on, and suddenly you realize you haven't thought about them for weeks. And when you do, it hurts.

The pain no longer tinged her every waking moment, for which Hattie was thankful. She had so many pleasant memories with her parents, and they had done their best to ensure she was well provided for.

"The stud farm will pay its own way," her father had said once he had realized the old farming tenants would be insufficient. "You just need to know how to handle it. Have someone alongside you who knows what they're doing with horses."

Hattie's stomach lurched. A face appeared as she blinked at the pile of invoices. An unwelcome one. Edward.

She pushed the thought away hurriedly, but like the brightness of a candle sparking in the dead of night, the image left its imprint on her mind even minutes later.

"That means the grocer can be paid this week instead of next," murmured Hattie to herself, inscribing the detail in pencil on the ledger. "And that means..."

She had to stop, go back three pages in the ledger, and tot it all up again. That couldn't be right. Her sums were usually correct, but that simply did not make sense. It couldn't be.

It was only after Hattie had recalculated thrice that she allowed herself to believe it.

"Well, well, Hattie Godwin," she said to herself quietly, leaning back in her chair. "You'll be solvent in three weeks. In time for the new year."

It was an astonishing thought.

Why, just a few months ago, she was starting to despair if she could ever catch up on her debts. Everywhere she turned there was something she needed to do: the horse doctor had come for a difficult birth, there wasn't enough hay so she had to go begging to a neighbor, a whole raft of meat spoiled in the larder and had to be replaced…

And then the roof had sprung a leak.

Hattie shook her head with a wry smile. Never before had she encountered such a run of bad luck.

But she had done what she'd always done. She'd put her best foot forward. She'd called the horse doctor and saved the foal. Gained a favor from her neighbor she'd promised to repay. Bought additional meat from the butcher and used credit with the grocer.

She'd even attempted to plug the leak in the roof herself, before he…

Hattie cleared her throat, as though that could clear the thought of Edward from her mind. It didn't.

Worst of all, she was led to compare the spineless, insipid man to another gentleman in her acquaintance. A gentleman who had far more interesting conversation. Far broader shoulders. And kissed…

"The accounts," she said firmly aloud. "The accounts!"

Hattie forced herself to look at the ledger. She had paid off almost all the debts. Another two weeks and the red column—the predominate one for the last six pages—would be empty.

And then, goodness. The black column could start to fill.

A strange sort of giddiness rushed through Hattie's chest. *Solvent? Already?*

She could never have imagined she would successfully turn the stud farm around. At least, she never would have done if she had been forced to do it alone. A certain fifty pounds a month had been an absolute godsend. And before long…

Hattie picked up the quill she always used on the ledger once she had ascertained her pencil calculations were correct. She twirled it in her hands, watching the glint of blue and purple in the soft feathers. The way the sunlight poured through the window before her, catching the colors, sparking them to life.

"Before long, my girl," Hattie said severely, "that income will be gone. He'll be finished, he'll have learned everything he can, and he will dispose of you."

"Dispose" was a harsh word, but Hattie had to face the truth. She was a servant of the Duke of Wincham.

Oh, they had shared kisses. For a moment, in the folly, Hattie had been certain the kisses had meant something. They had certainly meant something to her.

But Joseph's swift assurance that they would never speak of them again, never discuss it or even hint at it, told her what they truly meant to him. Very little.

Even if she could not get the sense of his arms around her from her mind.

And a pain, one Hattie had never felt before, seared through her heart. Joseph would be leaving her—at least, he would no longer require her services. Their acquaintance, friendship, whatever it was, would be at an end.

He had made it perfectly clear she was not a social equal. She had never been invited on one of these Wincham hunts, had never been invited to take tea with the late duchess.

So, Hattie told herself firmly, *you may care about him. Perhaps you care about him too much. But that doesn't mean he has any interest in you. In fact—*

"Goodness, I never would have pictured you holed up somewhere like this," said an unexpected voice from the open doorway.

Hattie started. The quill drifted to the desk, the ledger was snapped shut through instinct alone, and she whirled around to see—

Joseph. Standing in her study doorway. Leaning against the doorframe with a nonchalance that beggared belief.

How did he do it? Was it something about being a duke?

"What are you doing here?" Hattie said, words rushing from

her lips before she could consider how respectful, or not, they were.

Joseph appeared to delight in how taken aback she was. "Can't a neighbor pop in—"

"You have never popped in to see any of your neighbors," Hattie said severely, regaining some of her equilibrium and smirking as he gaped in astonishment.

"How very dare you!" said the Duke of Wincham with a laugh. "I—well, I…the fact remains—"

"You haven't broken into my house, have you?" asked Hattie easily, slipping into the teasing tone so natural between them now.

It was hard to remember that just weeks ago, she had berated him loudly for his inadequacies, and they had argued about her suitability to teach him to ride again, Hattie thought with a flash of mirth.

Goodness! If she could see them now…

"Broken into your—the front door was unlocked, I'll have you know!"

Hattie snorted. "And do you typically go around the neighborhood testing front doors to see if they are unlocked?"

In truth, she was glad to see him. They had finished their last lesson in such a rush, the rain coming down so rapidly, they had not agreed on when their next meeting would be. Not knowing had somehow cast a damper on her spirits.

Yet here he was, just two days later.

Joseph was still grinning. "I've surprised you. Good."

Hattie raised an eyebrow as her stomach twisted. Did he have any idea what he was doing to her? Could he possibly guess how she felt about him?

"You wanted to surprise me?"

"Well, you have surprised me so often, and impressed me, I'll admit," said Joseph, his debonair attitude suddenly fading. "It was rather pleasant to surprise you for once."

Hattie swallowed her instinct to tell the Duke of Wincham

she had never been more surprised at a man other than him.

Not just when she had realized it had been the duke himself she had berated so viciously. No, he was…resilient. Proud, yes. In pain when they had first met, though her ministrations and his obedience in adjusting his gait had solved much of that.

But there was something about him. Something that impressed, whether one wanted to be impressed or not. He was determined, striving to get better, be better. And yes, he had wallowed for a time. But who wouldn't after a catastrophe like what he had suffered?

"Now, are you going to show me around this place or not?"

Hattie blinked. Joseph was still standing in the doorway, his hand lightly holding his crutch as he leaned most of his weight on the doorframe.

Show him around?

"What on earth do you want to be shown around for?" Hattie asked, honesty tumbling from her lips before propriety. "I mean, your house is far more—I mean, nothing here compares to…it's just, you live in Cedarworth Lacey."

She had finished rather aimlessly, and her cheeks burned as Joseph met her gaze.

"Yes, I do," he said with a nod. "But I didn't actually mean your house."

Hattie frowned. What on earth could he—?

"I meant the stud farm," said Joseph with a shrug. "It's not something I've ever seen before. I thought—"

"Oh, of course!" Hattie said eagerly. She rose so swiftly from her seat that a handful of the invoices she'd been balancing in her lap cascaded onto the floor. "Oh, bother—"

"Here, let me—"

"No," said Hattie sharply.

She had not intended her words to be quite so defensive, but panic had spread through her chest like wildfire at the thought of Joseph seeing them.

There was no shame in debt, Hattie had always told herself.

But that didn't stop the feelings. One couldn't out-argue emotions.

Joseph did not move as Hattie's fingers quickly scrabbled to pick up the offending papers. Stuffing them in a drawer in the desk, praying she would remember tomorrow where she had put them, she straightened up and beamed.

"So. A tour of the stud farm. Where would you like to start?"

Joseph shrugged. "I have no idea."

Hattie decided to start at the most adorable end of the scale. That way, if Joseph grew tired, he would have a favorable impression of the place.

"Oh my goodness," Joseph breathed.

Hattie grinned. This particular barn was small, but it didn't need to be that large. Not for its inhabitants.

"There he is," she said softly, perching on a bale of hay just to the right of the door. "Let him come to you, if he's willing. It never bodes well to rush them. They don't like it."

Hattie had never met a foal comfortable with strangers in its home, but Joseph seemed to know precisely what to do. He crept forward just a foot then allowed himself to gracelessly collapse onto the straw-strewn floor.

Thunder, named by Hattie in a fit of pique when the brute wouldn't come without the horse doctor's intervention, nickered as he half staggered, half trotted over to the strange creature which appeared to be making its home in his straw.

"There now, Lightning," breathed Hattie quietly as its mother looked over to see who was approaching her baby. "It's just the Duke of Wincham. We can trust him."

She caught Joseph's eye and grinned.

Joseph said not a word. His attention swiftly returned to the long-limbed foal, which had swiftly reached him and was curiously sniffing him all over.

"He's beautiful, Hattie," Joseph said softly, gently reaching up a hand to pet the fuzzy little thing. "How old is he?"

"Just a few months, and an absolute terror he is already turning out to be," she said dryly.

There was something strange happening in her stomach as she watched the tall man become soft clay in the foal's hands. Joseph appeared to be utterly transfixed—*just as anyone should be,* Hattie told herself, *in the presence of a foal.*

Still. Something in her ached as she watched them.

"And what's his name?"

"Thunder," Hattie said with a gentle laugh. "I was irritated with him when he arrived; he gave his mother quite a difficult time."

Joseph chuckled. "I can understand that. How long will you keep them in here?"

"Oh, not long—they have grazing time every other day to ensure he stretches his legs, grows strong, and his mother doesn't grow frustrated with being cooped up here," Hattie explained.

The horse lore tripped off her tongue easily. She knew her craft.

"And your other mare doesn't bother him?"

"Technically, she's his aunt, but no, she doesn't bother him," Hattie said with a smile. "I've got over forty horses here after all, and—"

"Forty—did you say forty horses?"

Joseph's astonishment had raised his voice and the foal jerked back, startled by the sudden volume. Lightning lifted her head from her grazing to glare reproachfully at the duke.

"Sorry," whispered Joseph, raising his hands in surrender. "I didn't mean to—"

"Oh, he'll come back to you," said Hattie. "He's too curious not to."

They sat in companionable silence for a few minutes as she was proven right. Thunder may have returned to his mother's warm comfort as he attempted to understand what the odd noise had been, but the foal was far too nosey for his own good. Before another minute was gone, he had returned to Joseph, nickering softly at the strange creature.

"Forty horses," Joseph said softly as he reached out and patted the foal's neck. "I had no idea! Where did you get them from? How do you manage them all here on your own?"

Hattie swallowed. She had told herself she would not tell anyone—it was safer that way, to keep that particular part of her life secret. She had paid Edward back.

And besides, she had called the whole thing off. She didn't owe Edward anything, not anymore. There was no reason for Joseph to know, she debated silently. By the time she had managed to explain the whole thing, it would be over—and then there would be no point.

"I have two stable lads," Hattie said aloud.

Joseph's eyebrows raised. "So do I, and a stablehand—"

"I would call Mr. Knowles a stable lad," she quipped before she could stop herself.

His eyes danced with mischief. "I'll be sure to let him know your opinion. No, it was more that I meant—well. I only have nine horses. I thought nine rather a lot, considering I am hardly ever here. But forty?"

"This is a stud farm, Joseph," Hattie said, feeling a little sorry for the man. It was almost as though he had no idea what it was to make a living from these magnificent creatures. "I wouldn't make enough to live on if I didn't have sufficient mares, enough stallions to keep them breeding. I have three foals at present."

"Three?"

"Thunder is the baby. He's got a half-brother that's five months older, and a cousin, I suppose, who is a year older." Hattie squirmed in her seat on the hay bale as Joseph looked at her in wonder. "It's a busy old place, this."

"Yet you have taken the time to work with me," Joseph said quietly, his arm now around the gentle foal. "You must have had to work longer hours here to get everything done."

Hattie pushed her hair back nervously as she considered his words, wishing to goodness she had tied her hair up that morning.

It had certainly been difficult. Getting up earlier, staying up later. Trying to keep a closer eye on the stable lads as they were given more responsibility. But really, it was part and parcel of having a stud farm, Hattie had always thought.

Besides, she couldn't ignore the slight defensive surge in her chest. Did he think her incapable?

"You don't think I can manage this place?" Hattie said, trying to keep wariness from her tone.

"Well…no, I suppose I didn't," Joseph said unexpectedly.

His dark eyes met hers. There was something strange in them. A look Hattie could not fathom. A desire—no, not a desire. It wasn't quite affection either. Something different. Something in between.

"But the more I've gotten to know you, Hattie Godwin, the more I realize there's something unusual about you," said Joseph slowly. "It's like…well, I don't know how to describe it. I don't know how to describe you."

Heat flushed through Hattie. She wasn't sure if that was a good thing or a bad thing.

"I know the way you care for animals. Particularly horses," Joseph continued. "And now that I feel I know you better, why…I am surprised it's not a little bigger."

Hattie chuckled, hoping she could hide the astonishment at his praise. It was odd. Though she had not asked for it, she was remarkably pleased to receive it. Being praised by Joseph caused an outpouring of pleasure to ripple through her.

As long as she could keep the debts a secret, and Edward…

"I should probably let you get back to work," Joseph said ruefully.

"But you haven't seen the rest of the stud farm yet!"

"I know, but I would imagine you have work to do, and I would not wish to be a reason to keep you up late at night," said Joseph, pulling himself up on his crutch.

Her cheeks flamed with heat. *He did not mean it like that*, Hattie told herself sternly. *It was just a coincidence that it sounded like—*

"Now, what are you doing for Christmas Day?"

Hattie blinked. She had heard all the individual words, but together they did not make sense. "I beg your pardon?"

"Christmas Day," Joseph repeated, stepping over to her with a wry smile. "It's the day after tomorrow. Don't tell me you've lost all track of time."

Hattie hadn't. There were debts to be paid on Christmas Day, and against all the odds, she had paid them in time. But as to the day itself? She hadn't given it much thought.

"I'll be here, I suppose," she said aloud.

Joseph raised an eyebrow. "Alone?"

Hattie nodded. Why was he—?

"I'll be alone too, up at Cedarworth Lacey."

She snorted. "What, alone with your many servants?"

"I was going to ask you to come over for the day. Share Christmas dinner with me. But as you think I won't be alone…"

His voice trailed off as his dark eyes searched hers, and in that instant, Hattie knew—or at least, guessed—what he was asking. And it wasn't anything to do with roast goose and all the trimmings.

Mouth dry, heart hammering, Hattie did the only thing she knew how. "I accept."

CHAPTER THIRTEEN

December 25, 1810

"AND YOU'VE MADE sure that the red wine—"

"Has been breathing since breakfast was sent up, Your Grace," said Coulter with a reproachful air.

Joseph barely noticed. He was striding back and forth around the dining room, his crutch seemingly absent he was moving so smoothly.

He looked down. No, it was there, tucked under his arm. Strange. He had moved so quickly, so easily, he had half-forgotten it.

But he couldn't think of that now. Hattie would be here within the hour and the whole place was a disaster. What had he been thinking, inviting someone as important as her to his house—with only a few days' notice?

"These forks aren't clean," he snapped, his gaze darting to the dining table.

The dining table of the Winchams was, in Joseph's mother's words, a monstrosity. Designed for a visit of one of the great Stuart kings, though he could not remember which, the heavy wooden table was at least thirty feet long and designed to seat over fifty guests.

When set out for two, the thing looked ridiculous.

"The forks, Your Grace?" repeated his butler faintly.

Joseph did not know what made him say it. The gleaming silver forks looked well enough to him, but it was a convenient thing to latch onto. This, at least, he could berate.

"Absolutely outrageous, I don't know what you were thinking, laying them out here as though they were clean," he said darkly. "Take them away! Replace them!"

The butler did not say a word. Instead, Coulter's gaze met that of an underfootman.

Without speaking, the underfootman obeyed the silent order. He stepped forward, removed the offending forks, and swiftly replaced them with six new ones from the silver canteen.

Joseph looked down. He didn't really know what he was looking for. There hadn't been anything wrong with the originals.

No, there was something wrong with him. There was a most unpleasant churning in his stomach which did not appear to be quieting no matter what he did. No matter what orders he barked. No matter how many forks were replaced.

"Be off with you," he snapped.

The underfootman glanced over Joseph's shoulder at the butler.

"What, you don't take orders from me anymore?" Joseph bellowed. "I said leave!"

Hating himself, as though he was watching himself from outside his own body, Joseph continued to glare until the door to the hall shut behind the unfortunate underfootman.

His breath was ragged. When had he run out of breath?

"I hope the forks are now satisfactory, Your Grace," came the irritatingly calm voice of Coulter.

Joseph whirled around. "The goose?"

"Slowly roasted since yesterday, Your Grace, just as you like it," said the butler.

"And the potatoes?"

"I have been assured by Cook that they will be sufficient."

"And Knowles, he is aware—"

"A stall has been prepared for Miss Godwin's mount," Coulter said with a slight sneer. "Though a true lady would have come in a carriage."

That, at least, made Joseph's lips twitch.

Yes, he supposed he was right. Hattie was ignoring all of society's decorum by not arriving at a duke's home for dinner—*Christmas dinner*—in a carriage, but on the back of a mare. But then, what choice did she have?

"Miss Godwin does not have a carriage," Joseph pointed out.

His butler raised an eyebrow. "Your mother would have offered the young lady our own carriage. To pick her up and return her home."

Joseph opened his mouth, hesitated, and closed it again.

Blast it all to hell. She would have. Now why did that not occur to him? He could have shown a little chivalric pride. Actually done something for Hattie for a change.

As it was, Hattie had informed him cheerfully and without any opportunity to disagree that she would ride over on Bramble, as long as there was a stall in the stables prepared.

Joseph's shoulders slumped. "Ah."

"I think you will find, Your Grace, that all preparations which can be made, have been made," his butler said severely. "And if you will excuse me, I shall ascertain—"

"What about entertainment—is the pianoforte tuned? Is there a deck of cards laid? Are there any novels—?"

"Your Grace!" exploded Coulter in a most uncharacteristic display of frustration. "I know what I am doing! I have been the Wincham butler for nigh on thirty years, but if you think you can do a better job, may I suggest that you do it yourself!"

Silence fell between them. Silence, that was, other than the ringing words in Joseph's ears.

"I have been the Wincham butler for nigh on thirty years, but if you think you can do a better job, may I suggest that you do it yourself!"

His butler was staring in abject horror. Evidently the man had been pushed beyond breaking point. And it had been he who had done such a thing.

Why on earth was he so on edge? Why did he feel this desperate need to prove himself—no, not merely himself, but his home? His staff, his food?

Why, a voice muttered at the back of his mind, did he see the need to demonstrate to Hattie Godwin that he could…provide?

"Y-Your Grace—I-I—"

"And how long," Joseph asked dryly, "have you wished to say that?"

For a moment, his butler stood, face flushed, gaze averted. It was evident the man was mentally packing his bags and preparing to apply for a new position. Joseph could see it.

And the ridiculousness of it all cascaded through his mind. Joseph laughed.

Coulter's head jerked up, astonishment on his face as Joseph chuckled, his sides hurting he was laughing so much.

"A…a long time," admitted the butler dryly. "I am sorry, Your Grace, I don't know what came over me!"

"Oh, I wouldn't worry about it, old man," said Joseph, grinning at the dumbfounded servant. "I am beginning to discover for myself that it's better to get things out rather than bottle them in. Best foot forward and all that."

"Y-Yes, Your Grace," stammered Coulter.

"Please, go about your duties, and ignore me as much as you are able," Joseph said, shaking his head at his own foolish behavior.

His butler was staring as though he had been ordered to take a week off. "Right, I—"

"And apologize for me, will you?" called Joseph as the butler half walked, half staggered to the door. "I did not mean for my temper to get the better of me. A half-crown for everyone, in addition to their Christmas box."

Now Coulter's eyes were bulging. "R-Really, Your Grace? Oh, thank you—"

"That will be all, Coulter," Joseph said kindly.

The man was still stammering in the hallway. Joseph could hear him through the door.

Letting out a long, slow breath, Joseph reached out a hand to grasp the back of a chair.

Well, he had done all he could. The place was as ready as it would ever be for the arrival of a woman who had become such a shining light in his existence.

Not a day went by when Joseph did not think of her. Indeed, a day without Hattie's presence was fast becoming a day ill-spent.

And now she would be here, on Christmas Day.

Joseph swallowed. He wasn't sure why, but there was something in that. Something powerful. Something about sharing this particular day that felt more intimate than others.

Besides, their acquaintance, or whatever it was, had never extended to a meal. They had ridden together, talked for hours, sat in his library once. They had watched Thunder prance about with his mother, Joseph thought with a warm smile, but this…this was different.

This was how society would expect them to interact, he could not help but think. And they had managed to avoid it.

Until now.

The ringing bell made him jump. "What the—?"

Footsteps in the hallway echoed. *That was Coulter*, Joseph thought as panic rose in his chest. *And that meant—*

"Ah, Miss Godwin," came the butler's voice. "Ah, I see you are wearing—"

"Yes, thank you, Mr. Coulter," came Hattie's swift retort. "In here, is he?"

Joseph stumbled as he tried to walk around the ridiculously long table to meet her at the door, but his feet weren't quite working properly. He stumbled, regained his balance and kept walking, crutch supporting him on his left side, but before he could reach the door—

"There you are," said Hattie brightly as she stepped into the dining room.

And that was when Joseph fell.

In a spill of shock, confusion, and embarrassment, Joseph slipped to the floor, his leg unable to hold him at the sight of the woman who had just entered the room.

It couldn't be.

Lying on his back, head spinning, Joseph blinked up as that woman peered over him.

"Oh dear," Hattie said matter-of-factly. "Would you like an arm?"

There was no possibility of Joseph speaking. All the breath had been taken from his lungs the moment he had seen her, and the fall had knocked out the rest.

So in silence he grasped Hattie's warm hand and allowed himself to be helped.

"Here, let me," Hattie said in a rush of silk.

Joseph stared as she moved to pick up his crutch and offer it to him.

She blinked, cheeks starting to pink. "You're staring."

"You're beautiful," Joseph breathed.

It was all he could think to say, and it certainly didn't do her justice. For the first time in his life, Hattie was standing before him in a gown.

And not just any gown. This was a dark crimson gown of fine silk. It seemed to glide across her body like water, highlighting some parts, teasingly hiding others. Her breasts swelled in the bodice and she had done something to her hair. Joseph could not tell what, but the curls were elegantly piled on the top of her head, two curls drifting down either side of her eyes.

And her eyes…

They sparkled with more brilliance than a diamond ever had. Joseph was transfixed.

"Oh, you like the gown?" Hattie said, nervously smoothing her hands over the skirts. "I thought, you know, Christmas Day, one should—"

"I like you," Joseph said with a wry smile. "The gown suits."

He shouldn't be saying this. He knew how dangerous it was to teeter on the edge of admitting his feelings for her, and he had promised himself he would say nothing until the new year. That was when he would rid himself of Hattie's services as a horse trainer, and hope she would accept the far greater challenge of…

But now, seeing her like this—it was hard to remember there was a plan.

Hattie's flush was deepening, starting to match the rich color of her gown. "Do you have to stare like that?"

"Yes," Joseph said resolutely.

They stood for a moment in silence, him drinking in the sight of her, Hattie allowing him to look. Did that mean she would allow him to—?

"Shall we bring out the first course, Your Grace?"

Joseph turned to see Coulter had somehow managed to appear within the room. How long had he been there?

Now it was his turn for crimson cheeks. "What? Oh, yes. Very good."

It was a good thing Joseph had been taught his manners well, for he ran on pure instincts for the next hour. As food was brought out, red wine was poured, and candles were lit, daylight swiftly disappearing, Joseph found himself entirely enchanted.

The Hattie Godwin that sat beside him—they decided he would sit at the end of the table with her at his right—was not a completely different creature from the one he knew.

This Hattie laughed like that one, jested with him like that one. She certainly knew her horses, discussing with him some of her ideas for the stud in the new year. A stallion she wished to purchase, a mare she was considering selling.

"And you might be back in France this time next year," she said.

Joseph jolted. He supposed he might. It was a heady thought, but there was nothing keeping him in England, not now that he could walk and ride with the best of them.

Perhaps one thing held him here.

"Maybe," he said before changing the conversation.

Yet as Joseph watched her delicately raise a wine glass to her lips and giggle at one of his poor jokes, he realized this was another side of her.

He had seen the horse-loving, vibrant, defensive Hattie. The one who always spoke her mind and didn't care a jot what anyone thought. This was a more delicate, more intimate Hattie. A Hattie that flushed in the candlelight as he once again commented on her beauty.

"You're just saying that to be polite," she said with an arched eyebrow.

Joseph shook his head, unable to take his eyes from her. "No. No, in truth, if I were more polite, I would stop staring."

"You are, aren't you?" Hattie said softly.

Joseph swallowed, gaze darting to his untouched ice cream his cook had been so proud to present. But the delightfully cold confection could not attract all his attention, not now that he was seated with Hattie.

She was magnificent. Everything he'd thought he knew about her was being swiftly rewritten. True, he greatly admired her in breeches—what gentleman would not want to see the delicate shape that Hattie presented in them? But this feminine Hattie, one who had evidently gone to a great deal of effort for her appearance…

For his sake? Joseph wished it were so. Who else could it be for?

"Anything else, Your Grace?"

Joseph did not look round at the butler. "Nothing, Coulter. In fact, please would you let the servants know we are to be left alone; there will be no need to collect dishes until the morning. Miss Godwin and I have a few things to discuss."

Hattie smiled mischievously, teasing a wine glass around and around in her fingertips as the butler quietly shut the door. "Goodness, that sounds like you have business to discuss. You don't want to buy a mare, do you?"

Joseph grinned awkwardly. "No. Not quite anyway."

Oh, that was a terrible way to begin! What had he been thinking?

The thing was, thinking wasn't something he appeared to be particularly good at, not at the moment. Though he had drunk very little wine, all his senses were inebriated with her.

He had spent too much of his life repressing his feelings. Repressing true desires. Repressing the truth of his name and character in France, repressing the pain of his injury, repressing the injured pride which had been nothing but an anchor around his only remaining foot when he was recovering.

Joseph swallowed. And now he was repressing something else. Something that had absolutely everything to do with the woman just to his right.

Her hand was resting on the table. It was so close to his. If he just leaned forward—

"Well, I do have a few clients who rent a mare from me for a season," Hattie said, removing her hand from the table and placing it in her lap. "If they have their own stallions, I mean. Were you thinking of breeding from Maximus?"

Joseph's head was spinning. He did not want to be talking about horse breeding!

Yet it was so difficult, somehow, to turn the conversation to what he actually wished to speak of. The instant he started to think of it, his stomach lurched, his heart rate soared—

"That isn't what you meant, is it?" Hattie said softly.

Joseph forced himself to meet her gaze, and his need for her roared up into his chest. There was no one like Hattie. He had never thought to be so intoxicated with a woman who only did what society expected of her half the time.

If he was going to have any chance with her, though, Joseph told himself firmly, he could not be a coward. He had to speak up.

He had to, he thought wryly, obey her sound advice, and put

his best foot forward. Metaphorically.

"Hattie," Joseph said quietly.

Hattie's lips quirked. "Joseph."

"There is something I—not want, exactly..." He swallowed. Oh blast, this had already gone so wrong. How did other men speak so seductively to ladies?

When he had wanted to warm his bed, he had just found a woman. Procured one, you could almost say. And she would do her business, and he his, and she'd be gone in the morning.

No emotions ever came into it.

And now he was faced with the woman who had drawn from him the deepest emotions he had ever experienced, and—

"I know we said we would not talk of the folly," Joseph said, words slipping out.

As he had expected, Hattie's cheeks tinged pink. "Oh. Oh, I—"

"But I must," said Joseph, barreling on. If he didn't get it out now, he never would. "Because I—I care about you, Hattie."

For a moment, he held his breath, hardly daring to look. His heart sank as Hattie placed her hand on his and nodded. "And I care about you, Joseph. You're a good man."

Joseph pulled away his hand in an instant. "Don't give me that—that placating look! I'm trying to tell you I'm in love with you, goddamnit! I'm trying to tell you I want nothing more than to be with you, to have you in my bed, by my side at all times—I'm trying to tell you that I need you, that I want to marry you!"

And silence fell.

Chapter Fourteen

"DON'T GIVE ME *that—that placating look! I'm trying to tell you I'm in love with you, goddamnit! I'm trying to tell you I want nothing more than to be with you, to have you in my bed, by my side at all times—I'm trying to tell you that I need you, that I want to marry you!"*

Hattie could not help it. At the sound of those words—those passionate, unexpected words—her jaw dropped.

Heat rushed through her chest as longing and desire and all the affection she had carefully pushed aside since Joseph invited her to spend Christmas Day with him rose up.

"I'm trying to tell you that I need you!"

And although it was quite clear what the duke meant—if he had not spoken, Hattie had seen it in his eyes—she was not sure she knew what to do with herself.

To hear such a declaration, to see the look on Joseph's face as he made it, to see the anguish in his expression, the repressed desire that had suddenly burst forth from his lips...

It was heady indeed.

Hattie's head, in fact, was spinning. She had never expected...

Well, perhaps she had hoped. In the dark of the night, when her mind wandered back to the fervent kisses they had shared, she had wondered. When she had felt guilty about Edward, was certain she would have to tell him eventually, she hoped one day she and Joseph could speak so openly.

But to hear Joseph of all people bare his soul like that—

"You're staring at me," Joseph said dully. "It's fine, I understand. I never thought—"

"You are doing far too much thinking at the moment, and not giving me a chance to," Hattie said fiercely, embarrassment prickling her. "Just—just give me a moment, will you?"

She met his gaze. Perhaps something of her desperation to settle herself was visible on her face. At any rate, Joseph pressed his lips together and nodded without saying a word.

Hattie placed her hands on the arms of her chair.

Well. She had wondered—no, hoped—Joseph felt that way about her. That the fiery desperation she felt in his arms was in some way reciprocated. That the kisses which had meant so much to her had also meant a great deal to him.

It was not often, after all, that one was kissed silly by a duke.

But this was so much more than that, wasn't it?

Oh, Hattie knew that as far as the *ton* would be concerned, she had done well. Not well: the best a woman could do. Half the ladies she had ever met had wondered about the Duke of Wincham. What he was looking for in a bride, if there was a way of catching him.

Hattie had snorted at their conniving ways when she had first officially come out into society. When the invitations dried up and her attention drifted back to the stud farm, she had ceased to care.

But she knew in the eyes of society, she had succeeded. She had captured the attentions and affections of a great man.

Hattie's gaze flickered from her empty plate to Joseph. Her heart twisted.

Joseph was not great, however, because he was a duke. In fact, Hattie was rather of the mind that his title had held him back for far too long. Joseph was great because of his kindness. His internal fury at things which were not going his way. The way he tried to learn, even battling his temper before her when she had been naught but a stranger.

"No, that is not a thank you, Wincham. Come on, how hard can it be for a duke to thank a lady?"

"Thank you."

Her lips quirked into a grin.

"I suppose that is a good sign," Joseph said dryly.

Hattie breathed a laugh, leaning back in her chair. "You think you can just say such things to me and not expect me to need to take a moment?"

"I'm trying to tell you I want nothing more than to be with you, to have you in my bed, by my side at all times..."

Joseph had the good grace to look bashful. "I did not intend, believe it or not, to just blurt it out like that."

Hattie nodded, heart pattering in her chest. But he had intended something, hadn't he? Was this all part of his plan, this dinner?

"I'm trying to tell you I'm in love with you, goddamnit!"

She swallowed. He was in love with her.

And though it was surprising, though she never would have presumed to expect such a declaration, Hattie discovered in her heart of hearts, she had known.

At least, she had known how she had felt about him. How she longed for him, admired him. How he did not compare to a single gentleman she had ever met. Particularly not...

Hattie pushed the thought of Edward aside as best she could. She was not going to let him interfere with this moment. *This is precious, and mine,* she thought darkly. *Edward is not going to interfere, not even from the depths of my thoughts.*

She looked up to meet Joseph's eye and melted.

"You...you're in love with me," Hattie said in amazement.

"For my sins," said Joseph with a wry laugh. "Honestly, I did not expect—"

"But you meant it, didn't you?" she asked urgently. It was vital she knew; she had to be sure. If she could just look into his gaze as he said it—

"Meant it?" Joseph repeated. "Damnit, Hattie, I've been trying not to say it for the last few weeks. Ever since that folly—"

"You said we weren't going to talk about those kisses," Hattie said, trying to keep the accusing tone from her voice.

Well. He had said that. And most difficult it had been, Hattie thought as she shifted uncomfortably in her gown.

Joseph sighed. "I only said that because I knew it would be almost impossible for me to keep my hands off you if we did talk about it."

A flush of heat, excitement, and something more rippled through Hattie. "Truly?"

He met her eye steadily. "Hattie, every moment with you is a torturous practice of holding back. Not saying how I feel, not touching—damnit, I am supposed to be a gentleman!"

"And I am a lady," said Hattie, her stomach swooping as she said the words aloud. "A woman on my own, with no…no protection."

Though the words were stilted, she had to say them. She could not, after all, permit the conversation to continue without reminding him of that fact. If Joseph was to attempt anything, alone as they were in the dining room, not to be disturbed…

"…let the servants know we are to be left alone; there will be no need to collect dishes until the morning. Miss Godwin and I have a few things to discuss."

Well, there was no brother to protect her. No father to guard her honor. No relatives at all, in fact, to make the Duke of Wincham ensure she was treated properly.

Hattie swallowed. There was only one man in her life, and she had done her best to be rid of him. Mostly. The last thing she would wish to do is run to him to beg for his assistance.

"I offer you my protection," Joseph said instantly.

Hattie grinned, almost laughing as she said, "You say that so swiftly."

"You think I haven't thought about this? Considered it from every angle?" he said softly. "Hattie, you underestimate me."

His words caused a shiver to rush down her spine. Perhaps she had, but no longer.

"I..." Hattie swallowed. She had to say this, no matter how awkward it might be. "I don't want to be your mistress."

Her gaze had flickered to her hands in her lap, but now it rose and met his—and Hattie was astonished to see Joseph looked rather affronted.

Well, if he was going to be offended by a mere mention of—

"I don't want you to be my mistress either," Joseph said blankly.

Hattie's heart sank. Oh. Well, there it was then. It was all very well for a man to declaim passion and all that, but if he couldn't even be bothered to take her for a mistress! She should have known. She should have expected this sort of nonsense from a duke, she told herself fiercely. Well, she would simply return to the stables, find Bramble, and—

"Hattie, when I spoke of my intentions, I spoke advisedly," Joseph said quietly. There was a strange lilt of mirth in his voice. "I said I wanted to marry you. Were you not listening?"

Hattie's mouth fell open. "B-But...you..."

Her mind whirled as it recalled Joseph's sudden outburst when she had refused to take his hand—refused to allow her emotions and desires to get the better of her only to be, as she had supposed, disappointed.

"I'm trying to tell you that I need you, that I want to marry you!"

He couldn't be serious. A duke didn't offer matrimony to a woman like her!

Hattie swallowed. "Y-You can't mean that."

"And why not?" Joseph said fiercely. There was a light in his eyes she had never seen. "I've never met a woman like you, Hattie, never—and I would be a fool to let you go. A fool!"

Excitement sparked up her spine. "Truly?"

"Hattie Godwin, if you do not agree to accept me, it shall go very hard with you," Joseph warned, standing so rapidly his chair tipped over.

A rush of heat swept over Hattie's chest as she similarly rose, turning her back to the table as Joseph moved to stand before her.

Oh, this was daring—he was speaking in a way Joseph had never sounded before. As though he desperately needed her, as though he would do anything to have her.

Why did that tone make the space between her legs ache?

"You can't speak to me like that," Hattie said, heart hammering as she jutted her chin up. "I'll refuse to be your horse trainer if you—"

"Refuse if you wish," Joseph growled, pushing aside her chair with his crutch and pinning her against the table. "You're fired."

Now her buttocks were pressed against the table and there was nowhere to go for his chest was pressed against hers—and Hattie found she had absolutely no wish to be elsewhere.

Hattie wetted her lips, reveled in the way Joseph groaned at the dart of her tongue. "Fired, indeed? Well, that means I am no longer in your employ."

"So it does," murmured Joseph, dropping his crutch to the floor and placing his now free hand on her waist.

The merest sensation of his touch was enough to make tingles spread across Hattie's chest. Oh, she could hardly bear it! How did he have such an effect on her—how was she supposed to think when—

"In that case, we have no reason to see each other again," Hattie breathed.

Joseph dipped his head so his lips were mere inches from hers. She could not help it. She leaned up on her tip toes, desperate to accept his kiss, but Joseph lifted his head just slightly to avoid her.

Hattie moaned. "Joseph—"

"You haven't answered my question," he said quietly, his breath warm on her neck as he carefully placed a kiss on her collarbone.

Her eyelashes fluttered, her eyes unable to remain open at the sensual kisses Joseph started to trail along to her neck. How was anyone supposed to think with such—?

"Yes," Hattie moaned.

Joseph halted his kisses, his lips only an inch from her ear. "What was that?"

"Yes," Hattie repeated, her hands gripping the table, the only thing still keeping her upright. "Y-Yes…"

"Yes what?" Joseph said, placing a delicate kiss just below her ear.

Hattie shivered, unable to ignore the rising ache within her. She heard the swift intake of breath as Joseph watched her, gloried in the way she had such an effect on him, and knew there was only one suitable answer to his question.

Forcing her eyes to open, Hattie tilted her head and looked directly into Joseph's eyes. "Yes, I will marry you."

He captured her lips with such ferocity that Hattie gasped within his kiss, adoring the closeness, the intimacy.

Her hands were splayed against his chest, Joseph now the only thing keeping her upright. Hattie's mind was whirling with new sensations, new pleasures as Joseph's kisses grew deeper, far more passionate than those they had shared in the folly.

Their breathing was becoming ragged and Hattie knew they had to stop, cease their eager and frantic kissing—for she knew where this would lead.

And she wanted it. Oh God, she craved him.

"Joseph," Hattie whimpered as his hands swept plates, cutlery, and wine glasses off the table before moving to her buttocks, lifting her only for a moment before placing her on the now empty table.

Somehow he had moved between her legs. Her knees had parted, Hattie knew not when, and it was wonderful to have him nestled her. The intimacy, the closeness was more than she had ever dreamed. He was everything, all her world, and she wanted more.

"Hattie," Joseph breathed, managing to cease kissing her for just a moment.

It was a moment too long. Hattie reached up, her fingers curling around the nape of his neck as she tried to bring his lips back to her.

"Joseph, kiss me—"

"I will," he said, panting with the seeming exertion of not kissing her. "But I want more. Much more."

"Then take it," Hattie said as her mind whirled but knowing it was what she wanted. "Take it. Take me, take it all."

And though she had never spoken such words before, let alone found herself in such a position with a gentleman, Hattie seemed to know what to do.

Her instincts overwhelming her, she did not break eye contact with Joseph as she slowly leaned back on the table, pushing the wine bottle away. It tipped over onto the floor, but Hattie paid it no heed. She was far more interested in the way Joseph's eyes were widening at the sight of her lying on the table.

Hattie tried to steady her breathing as her fingers scrabbled at her skirts. She just had to bring them a little higher; they were at her knees now. A little higher—

"Hattie, wait!"

She halted. Joseph had put out a hand to stop her, as though he did not trust his words would be sufficient.

Breathing heavily, desperate for his touch, Hattie looked up at the man she loved and felt a strange pang of…rejection?

"You…you don't want me," she said softly.

Joseph groaned as his head dropped, then lifted again. "Quite the opposite, Hattie, trust me, but—"

"Well I want you," Hattie said, knowing she would never regret this moment.

How could she? They were to be married. She and Joseph would be happy for the rest of their lives, so why not start it now? Why not let this moment be the beginning of forever?

"But Hattie, you don't understand—"

"I love you, Joseph." The words had sprung from her heart and swiftly made their way to her lips. Hattie couldn't understand, now that she came to think about it, why she had never said them before.

She loved him. She loved everything about him. The pain and the anger, the kindness and the softness. She loved the way he lived, the way he saw the world. The way he saw the beauty in nature and cared so deeply for her.

It appeared Joseph was just as astonished to hear those words as Hattie was to find herself saying them. "You love me?"

"Do you think I would be lying on a duke's dining table like this if I didn't?" Hattie said, her teasing air once more returning.

Joseph swore under his breath as his fingers scrabbled to the buttons of his breeches. "Hell's bells, Hattie—"

"I love you, Joseph," Hattie repeated, a teasing air in her breathless voice as she saw the effect it had on him.

"Blast it, will you let me concentrate on—"

"I love you, Joseph—"

"Hattie Godwin!"

And she gasped. It was hard not to when Joseph covered her body with his own, his fingers grasping her wrists and pinning them onto the linen tablecloth.

He kissed her furiously, his teasing tongue drawing pleasure from her Hattie could not have expected. Her back arched and their mingled moans and whimpers filled the room.

Finally, when Hattie thought she could not endure anymore giddy decadence, Joseph drew back and looked deep into her eyes. His breeches were unbuttoned, now pooling on around his boot, and his manhood—

"You don't have to—if you don't want me to see..."

Her voice trailed off as her cheeks pinked, but Joseph did not need her to explain.

He cupped her cheek. "One day. Soon. But not today. Ready?"

Hattie nodded, with no time to say anything but, "Joseph!"

Nestled between her legs as he already was, it took very little movement for Joseph to slip his manhood between her thighs and toward her secret place.

She had expected—well, Hattie wasn't sure what she had expected. Pain, perhaps. Discomfort, certainly.

But as her body swelled and ached, as it let him in and accommodated inch after inch of Joseph's manhood, Hattie felt nothing but sparking waves of pleasure.

"Oh, Joseph," she moaned, her eyelashes fluttering once more.

"I'm going to make this as good for you as I can, Hattie," Joseph breathed, his fingers moving to her breasts, teasing around her erect nipples through her silk gown before moving to her hips, holding her steady. "Just tell me what you want."

"I want—oh!"

Hattie could not bear it. She could hardly breathe; such pleasure was pouring through her body as Joseph slowly removed himself and plunged back in.

Was this lovemaking? How did anyone stop long enough to do anything?

"Hattie, God, yes," Joseph moaned as he thrust into her again, his fingers gripping tightly onto her hips. "Like that?"

"Yes, like that, please, more," Hattie whimpered, her fingers curling into fists, grasping the tablecloth as though that would hold her steady.

The rising pressure of carnal desire was building in her somewhere, she could not tell where, but at any moment she knew she would be pushed over the edge of oblivion and—

"Oh, Joseph, yes, yes!"

Her cries were matched by the shudders of her body as Hattie's entire being exploded with ecstasy. Pleasure as she had never known pulsed through her body, taking her captive and not letting go as Joseph plunged himself back into her.

"Hattie!"

His sudden thrusting changed tempo, rapidly increasing until he cried out her name for a final time and poured himself into her.

Joseph collapsed and Hattie pulled him to her, knowing he would need her to balance him after such exertion. They lay there on the dining room table entwined together, Hattie's body quivering with the recent pleasure.

"Well," she breathed.

Joseph tilted his head and kissed her full on the mouth. "Well."

"That was—"

"I know," he said with a laugh. "Turns out a man with only one foot can still be an impressive lover."

Hattie tapped him on the shoulder as pure happiness radiated from her. "I could have told you that in the folly."

"We'll have to go back there."

"And make love?"

"I want to make love to you, Hattie Godwin," Joseph said with a growl, pulling himself upright, "in every room in this house..."

Chapter Fifteen

December 26, 1810

JOSEPH ALMOST SKIPPED down the stairs the next morning. "Happy Boxing Day, Coulter!"

His butler gave him a wry look. "So it is, Your Grace. So it is."

Beaming, unable to keep his joy to himself, Joseph glanced about the hallway.

It was incredible to see the world was the same. After such an evening as he had experienced last night, after such a wonderful connection, after such honesty and pleasure…

To think, there were the same paintings on the walls. The same large rug in the middle of the hallway. The same old Coulter.

It was odd, truly, Joseph thought to himself as he turned on his heel, his crutch ensuring he did not fall. He had never noticed so much of his home before Hattie had stepped into it. It had just been…home. The part of his life that never changed, rarely altered.

Even the servants were the same. He had inherited them, as it were, after his father had died and he had seen no reason to terminate their employment. There had been Coulters caring for his family for three generations, Joseph knew.

Yet though nothing had materially changed, Joseph knew everything had.

"I'm trying to tell you I'm in love with you, goddamnit!"

A slow smile spread across Joseph's face. She loved him. He loved her. Had any man ever been so fortunate as to capture Hattie Godwin's gaze? Had any man been wise enough to realize just what a jewel she was?

"Yes, like that, please, more..."

Joseph shivered as the memory of that hedonistic moment replayed in his mind. It was most astonishing, in truth, that he had not immediately recognized Hattie as the precious creature she was.

Though perhaps he should not berate himself too much. After all, at their first meeting, Hattie had not even known who he was...

"Well, everyone knows the Duke of Wincham is never here..."

Joseph grinned. Dear God, to think what had changed in the last few weeks. Then, he had thought her an upstart fool who had ideas on horses above her station!

Now he couldn't imagine a life without her.

How long would they have to wait until they were married? Joseph had never considered it before. Why would he? He'd never met a woman who could entice so before.

A week? Two weeks? Surely not a month?

"I take it then that you enjoyed your Christmas dinner with Miss Godwin?"

Joseph almost stumbled as he turned hastily to look at his butler. "I beg your pardon?"

Although he had expected some sort of reproach in the man's face, it appeared his servant had no idea what had transpired between him and Hattie last night. The reference to the Christmas dinner, apparently, had been entirely innocent.

Joseph tried to force down his smile. Well, it hadn't been innocent at all last night...

"Yes, it was pleasant, thank you," he said as Coulter waited for his response. "Please congratulate the kitchens. Hattie—Miss Godwin and I were most impressed."

Blast. He hadn't intended to call Hattie by her first name, not aloud. Coulter's eyebrows had risen so high they almost disappeared into what Joseph suspected was a wig.

"Indeed," said the butler coolly. "You seem in remarkably fine spirits, if you do not mind me saying so, Your Grace."

Joseph beamed. What did he care if his butler knew he was happy? The whole world could know, as far as he was concerned. There was going to be nothing but joy and laughter for the rest of his life. He had decided.

Yes, he had been miserable for a time. But Joseph had enough of being miserable. Why not choose joy? Why not enjoy life? Why not find happiness with a woman who looked at him like the most precious, the most handsome—

"Your Grace?"

"I beg your pardon?" said Joseph, blinking rapidly.

Goodness, had Coulter been saying something? Had he truly become so lost in his thoughts that he had not noticed?

"I was saying, Your Grace," said his butler, with just a hint of reproach, "that you are in fine spirits."

Joseph nodded. He must think about sending over a note to Hattie as soon as possible. No, why a note? Why not ride over there to Godwin Place immediately? There was no need to hold back, no need to follow the rules of the *ton*.

They were near a hundred miles away from London, and besides, they were in love. They were going to be married!

"Yes, yes, very fine spirits," he said as the servant waited patiently. "Yes, a wonderful—"

"I remark upon it, Your Grace, merely because I noticed a similar expression on Miss Godwin's face last night," interrupted his butler, his eyes wide with meaning. "When I helped her into the carriage to send her home. Rather late it was, too."

Joseph tried not to grin.

Well, he should have expected it. After acting almost as a

recluse for months, it was little wonder his servants were curious about the peculiar relationship their master was having with the woman who was his neighbor and horse trainer.

Let them wonder, he thought with relish. He hadn't exactly discussed with Hattie precisely when and how they wished to tell the world of their mutual affection.

They had…well. More interesting things taking up their attention.

Joseph's fingers quivered at the memory of Hattie underneath him. Despite his fine words, they had not managed to make love in every room in the building. Of course not! The place had nigh on fifty rooms; it would have taken far more time than they had!

They had only managed four.

Still, he had no wish to be embarrassed, and by a servant no less. It might have been different if one of his friends from London were visiting and had made that sort of remark, but from a servant?

No, that was insupportable. He would have to make a point.

Delicately. He had never been particularly good at that.

"Well, I am glad Hattie—blast, that Miss Godwin enjoyed her visit here," Joseph said, cursing himself silently for once again using her name.

It hadn't gone unnoticed. Coulter was frowning.

Joseph drew himself up straight. Now, this could not be borne. It was all very well for his butler to have an opinion, to be sure. But that didn't mean *he* had to be subjected to it!

"It is a credit to yourself and the rest of the staff," Joseph said, emphasizing ever-so-slightly the last word. "It is your hard work that makes Cedarworth Lacey so welcoming for guests."

Whether or not his butler understood the slight reproof was uncertain. He did nod. "Indeed. I hope I did not step out of turn in ordering your carriage, Your Grace, but it was very late, as I said, when Miss Godwin returned home, and your mother—"

"Yes, yes, I know she would have sent the carriage in the first place," Joseph said with a sigh. "I suppose my manners were lacking in that area, Coulter. Thank you for supplying my deficiencies."

That, at least, got a smile.

"My pleasure, Your Grace," said Coulter with a bow. "I was pleased to do it. The Godwins have been neighbors of the Winchams for generations. Of course, I did think that would cease, but it appears the stud farm has been saved."

For a moment, Joseph merely stared.

"...it appears the stud farm has been saved."

Each individual word made sense. Perhaps in another context he would have understood.

But Hattie's stud farm was in no danger. She would have mentioned it, surely. They had spoken so openly on many topics. *Sometimes far too openly*, Joseph thought wryly. Perhaps that was why he felt so close to her after such a relatively short acquaintance.

But as he looked at his butler, there was no hint of falsehood in the man's eyes. He held Joseph's gaze steadily, as though waiting for a reply.

A reply? What in God's name was he supposed to say to that?

"Ah," said Joseph helplessly. His fingers tightened around his crutch, which suddenly felt unsteady. "Good. The stud farm, you say?"

"Oh, she would have lost it if she could not have paid off the larger debts by the new year," said Coulter sagely. "But, of course, you knew that, Your Grace."

Joseph's mouth was going dry and he was finding it harder and harder to stand upright.

Debts? The larger debts?

But Hattie had never mentioned...there had never been any reference to...

"What, all that money such a burden?"

His stomach churned. Well, there had been that one moment, but...and a few other discussions about money, yes, now he came to think about it.

But she had always been so open, Joseph thought quickly, his mind whirling. Hattie had never struck him as someone who hid anything. She was so unguarded, so blunt. In some cases, far too much.

Why would she hide this?

"I…yes, naturally," Joseph said slowly as his butler waited for him to speak. Why couldn't the blasted man go and polish something? "Hattie's debts were very small—"

"I would have said considerable, begging your pardon, Your Grace," said Coulter smoothly. "It's the talk of the village, as these things are. But your payments to her have made all the difference, and I hear she has disposed of almost all her overdue bills now."

Joseph stared, unblinking, as the words sank slowly into his mind.

His payments to her had made all the difference…

Well, he had known she was being paid. That was what they had agreed, he tried to tell himself. True, he had forgotten that the moment he had first stolen a kiss, but she evidently had not.

And though there was probably a completely reasonable explanation, though Joseph was certain if he spoke with Hattie she could immediately reassure him, panic and distrust started to flitter through his heart.

If he had known she was struggling so financially…

Would that have changed anything? Would it have altered the way he treated her? Would it, in fact, have made him more guarded?

"I thought you knew, Your Grace."

Joseph's head jerked up. There was a look of genuine contrition on the man's face.

He tried to smile. "Of—of course I did, Coulter. I merely—"

A loud jangle of the doorbell cut across him, halting their conversation.

Yet there was still a worried expression on the servant's face. "That will be Miss Godwin, I expect."

Joseph's jaw dropped. *Now how on earth did he know that?*

"I instructed Miss Godwin to return at about this time to collect her mare, you see," said the butler wretchedly, stepping over to the front door. "I did not think—because of the carriage, you see, and—"

"Yes, yes, very well, Coulter," said Joseph automatically, desperate to put the man out of his misery. "But don't you worry about that. I'll get the door."

He found himself striding forward before all the words had left his mouth. It was nonsense; no duke should be answering his own front door.

But the thought of standing in the hallway with Hattie and his butler after just discovering the truth about her debts…no, that could not be borne. *Better to get rid of the servant*, Joseph thought feverishly. Then he could talk to Hattie alone and…and…

And what? A dark, cruel voice muttered in the back of his mind. *You'll ask her, will you?* Whether she conspired with Doctor Walsingham to ensure herself a position? If she took on the role merely because she needed his money?

Well, that would not be so bad.

But if she had accepted his kisses merely because he was a wealthy man—if her affections were not due to himself but because of his ability to pay the remainder of her debts—

"Are you certain, Your Grace?" said the butler nervously, interrupting Joseph's thoughts. "It is not seemly, a duke—"

"That was the order I gave, Coulter," Joseph snapped, all the happiness of the morning melting away. "You would like to disobey it?"

The glare he gave the man was enough. Coulter bowed low and walked to the door that led to the servants' corridor. Only when it had closed did Joseph walk to the front door where Hattie was waiting on the other side.

He did not have time to think about what he would say. There was no opportunity to sit and reflect, wonder whether the raging panic that he had been duped was in any way valid.

Joseph wrenched open the door. "You," he snapped.

Hattie took a step back, her face flushed. "I—goodness, Joseph!"

She was so beautiful. It was a distracting thought, but not one Joseph could ignore. She was wearing breeches again, her riding coat tight around her and a knitted scarf around her neck, battling against the cold.

Her eyes were wide, clearly astonished that Joseph himself had answered the door.

"I-I walked over, you see, to collect Bramble," said Hattie into the silence, as Joseph merely stared. "Your butler said it was—"

"Come in," Joseph said firmly, stepping back to welcome her in.

For an instant, she hesitated. Was that because she knew? Joseph wondered hopelessly, his mind spinning with a thousand and one thoughts. Was it because she had only offered herself to him, only agreed to his requests, only accepted his kisses because it was financially prudent to do so?

Oh God, that he had allowed himself to be so used!

"Oh, thank you," Hattie said, stepping into the hallway. "It is so much warmer in here, thank you. I—"

"Tell me about your debts," Joseph said flatly as he shut the door.

A part of him hoped she would feign ignorance. Perhaps she was innocent, a desperate part of him begged. Perhaps there was a misunderstanding. Perhaps there was another young lady in the area who had racked up debts, perhaps—

But Hattie did not say anything. She did not attempt to defend herself or even ask him to repeat the question to give herself more time.

Instead, she slowly unwound the scarf from her neck and twisted it in her hands.

"What do you want to know?" she asked quietly.

Joseph's heart sank. It was true then. "How much?"

"Far too much for one stud farm to manage at the time,"

Hattie said with a forced brightness that grated on Joseph's nerves. "I had thought, at first, I could sell—"

"But you didn't," Joseph interrupted.

They were standing several feet apart, and though he wished to close the distance and pull Hattie into his arms, he knew he could not. If he did, he would forgive all, ignore all. Anything just to have her.

And he couldn't allow himself that pleasure.

He was the Duke of Wincham, Joseph reminded himself. He was owed some respect.

"No, I didn't sell any horses in the end," said Hattie softly. "I found work."

"You found me."

"It wasn't like that," she said firmly, voice strengthening as her gaze met his. "When Doctor Walsingham—"

"Is that all this has been?" Joseph said, his voice breaking as he took a step forward. "Is that all I am, a rich gentleman who can pay off your debts while you entertain him?"

"Joseph!" Hattie looked scandalized. "You really think what we have is for money?"

She sounded so horrified it was easy for Joseph to believe her. After all, Hattie had never been someone to hide her emotions. They were always there, plain as the nose on her face. One only had to look at her to know what she was thinking.

Which was why this was so difficult. Joseph had never seen Hattie look so wretched, so overcome with emotion.

"I love you, Joseph."

Joseph pushed the memory away. He had to know, had to be sure—

"You invited me here thinking I was a man and told me that I couldn't teach you a thing," Hattie began. Joseph winced at the memory. "I accepted the challenge of working with you. I admit, I needed the money—but there is no shame in that!"

"I did not wish to buy your affections," Joseph said curtly.

"And you didn't!" Hattie said passionately. Her cheeks were

still pink, but seemingly from the lust in her voice now rather than the cold wind outside. "Joseph, you think you were the only recourse I had to pay off those debts? Are you really so arrogant as to think there was no one else I could turn to, no other options before me?"

Joseph opened his mouth, hesitated, and then closed it again.

It was a point well made, even if he had not thought of it.

Hattie Godwin—the whole Godwin family—was well-liked and respected. There were surely plenty of people who could have helped her. And yet she had agreed to work for him.

And more.

"So…you never considered," he began awkwardly.

Hattie took a step toward him and Joseph almost moaned aloud at the desperate need to be closer to her. Oh, he was utterly lost. She could tell him anything now and he would believe her. He would want to believe her so desperately because she was just so…so…

So Hattie.

"If you had nothing but the money you could pay me, I would have worked for you," Hattie said calmly. "And if you had kissed me, I would have kissed you back. I did. And I would have kissed you in that folly, which I did. And when you put me on that dining room table—"

"Yes, yes," Joseph said hurriedly, glancing about. You never knew when a servant was listening… "I just—"

"You want me to love you for you," Hattie said simply.

Joseph swallowed.

It sounded so…so childish when she put it like that. But she was right. The idea that Hattie's affections were more focused on his wealth than him fed directly into his fears that he was no longer enough.

Not enough for Hattie because…because he had lost a leg.

Was he truly that shallow? Joseph prodded his emotions carefully, and found more complexity than he had ever considered.

He had not yet managed to untangle all his feelings toward the loss of his leg. Even now, he was not sure how he would be received in town, whether he even wanted to return. He knew he must return to France, but how, in what capacity, he could not tell.

But there was one thing he could be sure of.

"I thought I would lose you," Joseph said, his voice quiet. "If I lost the money."

And all of a sudden, Hattie was in his arms, and she was embracing him as though they were about to be parted forever.

"Joseph, I love you," Hattie said fiercely in an undertone, her breath tickling his neck. "You. Not your title, not your wealth—none of that matters. Can't you see that?"

Joseph clung to her. "I want to."

"Well then, I'm just going to have to spend the rest of our lives making sure," she said with a gentle laugh. "You still want to marry me, I presume?"

There was just a hint of uncertainty in her voice, and that was when Joseph realized.

She had been just as unsure about him. Perhaps, had even come to the house instead of going directly to the stables to ensure he still cared about her. That their lovemaking was not merely a physical release, but an emotional connection.

Joseph's arms came around the woman he loved and held her tight. "I will marry you."

CHAPTER SIXTEEN

IT WAS A relief, in truth, to be home.

Hattie's spirits rose as the familiar site of the old house and the stables which hugged three sides of it came into view.

"Almost home, Bramble," she said quietly, patting her mare's neck. "Almost home."

Sleep had not been high on the agenda last night. She'd had far more interesting things on her mind. And open to her. The way Joseph kissed…

She was not naïve enough to think she had been his first. He was a duke, after all. Dukes had their way with ladies, particularly if he had spent time in London and in France. As far as Hattie was aware, that was almost all they did in France. Make love and make war.

But despite that, her lovemaking with Joseph had felt incredibly special. As though they were discovering things together. As though it had been just as new and exciting for him as it had been for her.

"Turns out a man with only one foot can still be an impressive lover."

Hattie smiled, tiredness aching in her bones as her horse trotted toward the stables. There had been little opportunity to talk with Joseph about the future, and it was partly why she had gone up to the house to speak with him rather than straight to the stables.

After all, she knew Mr. Knowles would be looking after Bramble splendidly. It was her potential marriage with Joseph that needed to be checked on.

Not, Hattie thought with a jolt to her stomach, her marriage to Joseph. Her marriage to the Duke of Wincham.

Goodness. She hadn't considered that.

And after such a confusing conversation with Joseph, after realizing he thought she had only sought to win him because of his wealth, Hattie was exhausted. All she wanted was to put Bramble back in the stables, ensure Thunder and his mother were doing well in the small barn round the back, then head inside.

Head upstairs and straight to bed, Hattie thought ruefully as she glanced up at the sky. It may only be mid-afternoon, but it was already growing dark and she was dog tired. An early night would certainly do her no harm.

"You are certain you do not wish to stay here?" Joseph had asked almost half an hour ago as she had saddled up Bramble outside Cedarworth Lacey.

And Hattie had been tempted. It was pleasant, the idea of a hot bath—she hadn't had that luxury in a while. It was even more tempting to think of the pleasure she and Joseph could share together in the privacy of a real bedchamber.

But her horses had been calling her. She wanted to go home.

"Besides," Hattie had said to Joseph with a laugh. "You are about to spend the rest of your life with me, Joseph. You should take the chance to have an evening to yourself while you still can!"

His hand had rested on hers on the reins, and Hattie had been warmed by the instant connection between them.

"I will consider it an evening wasted," Joseph had said quietly. "Any evening without you is one sorely lacking. Be safe now, Hattie. It'll be dark soon."

Hattie smiled as she remembered the conversation. How had she been so fortunate as to attract such a man? The only other man who had shown any interest in her…

Well, suffice to say that she had been pleased to escape his clutches. There was absolutely no comparison.

The welcome snuffling of horses met Hattie as she entered the stable. Most of her studs were outside, enjoying what little grass they could eat. She'd have to remember to ask one of the stable lads to bring them in, Hattie thought as she dismounted from her mare and rubbed her nose. They only came for a few hours each evening now, not even bothering to knock at the house. Sometimes she could go a few days without seeing them.

"Did you miss this place, Bramble?" she asked quietly, smiling at the snuffles her mare made. "Yes, I thought you might."

It would be another thing she and Joseph would have to consider, Hattie thought as she slowly and gently removed the saddle and tack from Bramble. Where they were going to live.

Oh, it made complete sense to live in Cedarworth Lacey. The place was huge. It would be wrong not to move there when Joseph was so comfortable there.

Besides, Hattie thought with a grin, she could hardly imagine him growing accustomed to the relatively pokey rooms of her home.

But that didn't mean she would necessarily want him equally involved in her stud farm. No, there was a part of her that wanted to keep that separate. Wanted to prove to him, as well as herself, that she could continue to manage the place on her own.

"If only all my property wouldn't become his," Hattie murmured aloud as she started to rub down the mare. "It really is most unfair."

That was how it had always been. Why, she could hardly conceive of a world in which a woman could keep her own private property after marriage. It was impossible to think of.

What on earth would the ladies do with all that power?

It had been one of the reasons she had never wished to marry in the first place. At least, not to—

But Joseph was different, Hattie knew. Not just different from

Edward, but different from every man she had ever met.

"I thought I would lose you. If I lost the money."

To think he had been so concerned about her intentions toward him! Hattie had never heard of such a thing. After all, was it not common for fortune hunters to be blatant with their hopes? Were they not always seeking wealthy men? Had he not encountered that before?

"Perhaps that was why he was so worried, eh, Bramble?" Hattie murmured as she led the horse into her stall and closed the door behind her. "Perhaps he'd suffered through such a thing in the past."

It was a strange thought. Hattie rather hated the idea of Joseph falling in love with anyone else just to have his heart broken. In truth, she didn't like the idea of him falling in love with anyone else at all.

But as she breathed in the comforting smells of the stables, she knew the past didn't matter.

So much had happened in her life and Joseph was not the sort of man to hold it against her.

No, what was past was past. Hattie knew she couldn't worry about it, she could only think on the future. Put her best duke forward, she thought with a wry smile. And then—

Perhaps if she had not been so tired, she would hardly have noticed the strange sound. As it was, Hattie's nerves were already taut. Exhaustion from a night of lovemaking, the long walk from Godwin Place to Cedarworth Lacey, and the awkward exchange with Joseph had tired her out, and her senses were heightened.

So she did notice the strange sound.

Hattie turned around. All the horses in their stalls were quiet. None of them had been startled, yet she could have sworn she heard—

There it was again. It was not a completely alien noise. In fact, a few years ago it would have been heard around the stud farm all the time.

But she had sold the carriage to pay off the bulk of the arrears on an unexpected invoice some months ago. Hattie remembered seeing the old thing being driven away. It had been a bittersweet moment. That had been the carriage she and her mother had used to go visiting on the rare occasions they received an invitation. It had been like saying goodbye to a piece of her mother to see it go.

And that was definitely the sound of a carriage on the cobbles in the stable yard.

Hattie leaned against the stable wall for a moment, collecting herself. It truly was too bad that someone would come visit her unannounced—and on Boxing Day, too!

Well, there was nothing for it. She would have to go out there and attempt to be cordial. She would ask them to return in a week. When she had rested. When she would know precisely when she and Joseph were going to be married.

A spark of joy soared through her chest. Hattie smiled in the dark warmth of her stable.

Married, to Joseph. Oh, she could hardly wait!

But when she opened the stable door and looked out on the stable yard, the joy was replaced with horror.

It was no carriage, but a dog cart. There were two men around it, a driver, and a fourth sitting in the dog cart with a hat covering his face. The two in her stable yard were hastily tying bridles to the back of it.

Bridles attached to her horses. Lightning, and Thunder, and three others—

"Hie there!" Hattie called out instinctively, stepping forward. "What do you think you're doing?"

All thought for her own safety, all sense that she should hide, should be grateful they had not spotted her entering the main stable, flew from her mind. Hattie was thinking of nothing at all but her horses as she stepped into the fading daylight, heart pounding.

How dare they even think about stealing her horses!

The two men tying the horses to the dog cart whirled

around.

One of them swore. "Who in God's name—"

"It's her, the Godwin woman!" said the man holding the reins of the dog cart. "I thought you said she wasn't here!"

"I thought you said you would help," snarled the first. "Come on, we've got to—"

"You will do no such thing!" Hattie said, still striding forward.

Her chest was tight, lungs battling to take in air, but she was absolutely certain she could not allow these miscreants to steal her horses.

She had heard of this. It was a tale told by horse breeders to other breeders to spark panic, to increase security, to ensure there were always at least two men in the stables at all times.

And Hattie had always followed those rules.

Until she hadn't. Until paying the wages of so many men had become impossible, until the debts she was accruing made paying them a choice between them and feeding herself.

Hattie's gaze fell on the man who had remained silent. It was one of the stablehands she had been forced to let go. Perhaps the man still seated, face hidden, was another. Had she really deserved this?

"How dare you come back here and steal from me!" Hattie shouted, rage in her voice.

But somehow, her legs were not moving fast enough. She had never thought of her stable yard as large, and spending more time with Joseph and Mr. Knowles at Cedarworth Lacey had confirmed that.

Yet she seemed to be getting no closer. It was outrageous, what they were doing! Did they have no shame?

"You said she wouldn't be here," said the first man accusingly to the man Hattie now recognized as Walker.

"I said she shouldn't be, all right? Can't blame me, she lives here an' all," snapped Walker, his fingers fumbling. "We just have to—"

"No!" Hattie cried.

She had finally reached the men, but as her mind raced, she could not think what to do. There were four of them and only one of her, and each one of the men was surely stronger.

And so she did the only thing she could think of.

"Go away!" Hattie said, kicking the man who approached her as she desperately tried to free Thunder's bridle.

The little horse was panicked, neighing fit to burst, his cries agitating his mother.

"I know, I know," Hattie said feverishly. "I said go away!"

But this time, her foot missed the leg of the man approaching her so there was nothing to stop him from grabbing her.

Hattie cried out. "Let me go!"

But there was no one to hear her. The stable lads would not be back until dark, Hattie knew, to bring in the last of the horses and feed them their oats. The only house servant, a maid, had returned to her parents' for Christmas.

Hattie struggled, but Walker's grip on her was absolute, his strong arms pinning her own to her side. "Let me go, I'll tell—"

"There ain't no one to tell, so you scream all you like, missy," sneered the driver. "God's teeth, this is almost more trouble than it's worth!"

"I tell you, that foal will go for a pretty price to the Glasshand Gang," snapped the man still tying bridles to the dog cart.

Hattie continued to struggle, trying to wrench herself from the man who held her, but there was no use.

She watched, sobbing, as another two horses were tied to the back of the dog cart. Her stallion Mercury, and—

"You'll regret this!" she shouted before Walker clasped his hand over her mouth.

"Can't you get her to shut up?" asked the driver wearily.

Red-hot panic was flowing through Hattie's veins. She couldn't allow this to happen—she couldn't just watch as her precious horses were stolen from her!

It wasn't just that they were her life's work, the backbone of her stud, everything she had worked so hard to protect and keep.

They were also *hers*. Her horses. She had a connection with them like no other. She loved Joseph, yes, but these creatures depended on her, had been taught by her. She had been there when most of them had been born. The few she had bought, she had trained.

They were hers.

"Ye gods!"

Walker wrung his hand as Hattie tried to pull away.

"What the—"

"Did she bite you?"

"This little terror needs to be put in her place," said Walker firmly, starting to drag her away from the dog cart. "Come on, Miss Godwin."

Tears were flowing from her eyes as Hattie tried to drag her feet against the cobblestones, anything to stop him. She hadn't considered her own safety as she had rushed toward the men. The only thing in her mind at the time had been the safety of her horses.

She was thinking of herself now. What was going to happen to her? What would Walker do to her?

"No!" Hattie cried, twisting rapidly in his grip.

And somehow, she didn't know how, she managed it. Walker swore under his breath as she slipped from his tight clutches, and Hattie rushed toward the horses with one thought in her mind.

Pulling the knife she never thought she would have to use from its secret place in her corset, Hattie did the only thing she could think of.

"Run!" she screamed at the horses as she cut through the leather thongs the thieves had used to tie them.

Her horses did not need telling twice. Already filled with panic and confusion, the horses ran one by one into the lane, galloping off into the distance.

Hattie's heart ached as she watched them go, one after another, but she knew it was the only choice she had. Hopefully they would return to her, or they would be found and brought back. Everyone knew Godwin Place was the only horse farm for miles around.

But even if they didn't, running free had to be better than whatever these men had in store.

The driver was swearing. "Someone stop her!"

The man who had not yet revealed his face rose and jumped out of the dog cart as the two men who had been tying the horses jumped in.

"It's all over—let's get out of here!" yelled Walker, shoving the driver. "Just go!"

Hattie's heart leapt. *If they would just leave—*

"Go!" shouted the other man.

And although the hatted man was no longer in the cart, the driver snapped the reins viciously.

"You can explain to the Glasshand Gang then!" he cried as the cart moved away rapidly, pulled by their own horse, the only horse they were leaving with.

Hattie's chest was on fire, her breaths short and panicked, and it was only as the dog cart turned a corner in the lane and disappeared from sight that she realized she was not entirely free from danger.

The unknown man was still standing in her stable yard.

Hattie swallowed, shifting the knife in her hands and wondering…

Would she?

She had never been forced to face the decision before. Could she hurt a man? Would she use a knife against him, even though he'd done nothing but watch as her horses were almost stolen?

And then the man removed his hat, revealing a dark smile and a well-known face.

"Well, well," said Edward with a chuckle. "We do find ourselves in a predicament, don't we, Hattie, my darling?"

Chapter Seventeen

December 27, 1810

JOSEPH DID NOT consider himself a truly impatient man.

Oh, he grew irritated if his every whim was not catered to. That was part and parcel of being a duke; you demanded the best, even if the best was not immediately offered to you.

In many ways, he was patient. At least, that was what he told himself as he paced somewhat awkwardly around and around the entrance hall.

Joseph glanced at the grandfather clock. "Is that thing right?"

His bark echoed around the room and made the maid who had been dusting one of the gold gilt landscape painting frames start.

"Y-Your Grace?"

"That clock," Joseph snapped, pointing at the offending timepiece with his crutch. It was only because of Hattie, he thought painfully, that he could do so. "Is it the correct time?"

It was a simple question, yet the woman hardly seemed to know how to reply. "Y-Y-Yes, I th-think—"

"Go and get Coulter," he growled, resuming his pacing.

The maid scampered away and Joseph was left with his thoughts.

Hattie was late. It was not like her, although he would not put it past her to become distracted as she rode over, he thought with a wry smile. Or discover Thunder hadn't eaten enough, so stay with him an additional hour to ensure he did.

Yes, there had to be a reason she was not here by ten o'clock sharp.

"What?" Joseph snarled, whirling on his heel as a door opened.

His expression softened as his butler bowed low. "Your Grace, I was informed—"

"Is that clock right?" Joseph asked testily. He had no time for obsequiousness.

Coulter looked at the grandfather clock and Joseph mirrored him. Almost twenty minutes past ten o'clock.

"I did wind it only three days ago, Your Grace, on Christmas Eve," said Coulter slowly, approaching the grandfather clock and pressing his ear against the casing. "But if your pocket watch shows it to be slow, I will of course rectify the situation immediately."

Joseph's jaw tightened. Ah. He had forgotten his pocket watch.

Refusing to meet his butler's eye, he reached into his waistcoat pocket and pulled out the much smaller timepiece. His pocket watch said nineteen minutes past the hour.

"Hmmmph," said Joseph darkly.

When he looked up, Coulter had an eyebrow raised. "Well?"

"They concur," Joseph admitted. "So where is she?"

His butler raised his other eyebrow, the two disappearing into the potential wig. That was happening more and more often, Joseph noticed. Not a good sign.

"*She*, Your Grace?" Coulter said icily. "I cannot imagine who you—"

"You know precisely who I mean, man, come on!" Joseph snapped. "Hattie Godwin! We agreed she would come here at ten o'clock and—"

"And what, Your Grace?"

Joseph swallowed. It was rather unpleasant to receive the disdain of your own butler.

He understood why. It was not seemly, not appropriate, to be seducing ladies who came for Christmas dinner. It was even less seemly, and more than a little scandalous, to bed them on your dining room table.

He had attempted to tidy up as best he could. But Joseph was unaccustomed to such things. He was certain the footmen had guessed, and they would have shared their suspicions with Coulter.

No wonder the man was looking like…like that.

Joseph cleared his throat. "I am going to the drawing room. Send a footman when she arrives."

And without waiting for another word from his butler, he stormed off.

It was a long two hours that Joseph spent there, pacing just as he had in the hallway. He did not seem to be able to stand still. There was uneasiness in his chest that only settled when he was moving. The instant he halted, nausea rose up.

When the gong rang for luncheon, Joseph stomped into the dining room in a temper.

"She is not coming then, I take it?" asked Coulter delicately.

"Go to hell," snapped Joseph. "Go on, leave me, all of you!"

The startled footmen and an underfootman scampered swiftly. Only the butler walked sedately to the door and bowed before he closed it.

Joseph half sat, half fell into a chair.

This was ridiculous. The moment he did not have Hattie, his bad temper returned, his irritation at the world, frustration that nothing was going his way.

She had a calming effect on him, yes, but it did not last without her. He needed Hattie by his side. Their wedding could not come swiftly enough.

"She's just been caught up with something," Joseph muttered

as he served himself cold ham and potatoes. "She'll arrive tomorrow full of apologies and explanations."

And that was all the comfort he was to receive.

The next morning, Joseph rose early. Well, he reasoned, what if she wanted to go on an early morning ride? He hardly wished to disappoint her. And they hadn't quite mastered the way he hunted, not yet. Holding a gun in one hand was difficult when already imbalanced.

This time, he did not pace around the hallway.

"—and of course, we will need to air that set of bedchambers, they have not been used in—Your Grace!"

Joseph looked up, his head resting on his elbows.

Coulter appeared astonished. He had been walking across the hallway with Mrs. Alan, the housekeeper, evidently discussing matters of the estate.

Joseph supposed they had not expected to see their master seated on the bottom stair.

"You are not injured are you, Your Grace?" Mrs. Alan said, rushing toward him.

"Oh, away with you," Joseph said, waving a languid arm. "I am perfectly well. I'm just waiting for…I'm just waiting."

He didn't appreciate the way his two most senior servants exchanged knowing glances.

"And that's enough of that, I'm sure," he added.

Mrs. Alan's cheeks went pink. "So you are waiting for Miss Godwin then?"

Joseph was in half a mind to deny it, but what was the point? The whole world would soon know how he felt about Hattie. "Yes."

"And she still has not arrived?" said Coulter.

If Joseph wasn't mistaken, there was a worried tone in the butler's words. *Now that was new.* He shook his head.

"Well, that is rather strange," said Mrs. Alan. Then, as she saw Joseph's expression, she added hurriedly, "Unless of course, she believed her invitation yesterday rescinded because she was unable to call? Perhaps she is…I don't know, embarrassed. Uncertain whether she is welcome today."

Joseph considered this. It was an appealing thought. It would certainly explain why Hattie had not turned up today, bright smile and cheeks blazing pink after the exertion of riding in the dead of winter.

Still. It would not be like Hattie to be reticent. She was a woman, Joseph knew, who would happily turn up anywhere and merely assume she was welcome.

His stomach twisted painfully. "Nothing could have…have happened to her, do you think?"

"Nonsense," Coulter said smartly. "She's got two stable lads up there, and—what's her name, Mrs. Alan?"

"Betty," the housekeeper said promptly. "Our Sarah's sister, she works for Miss Godwin. You'd soon know about it, Your Grace, if something ill had befallen Miss Godwin. She has three people about her all the time. Most of the time anyway."

Momentarily relieved, Joseph nodded.

Yes, that was true. It was hardly as though Hattie was alone up there. They would have heard, a message would have been sent. Nevertheless…

Something did not sit right. There was something wrong, Joseph knew it. The trouble was Hattie would not thank him for just turning up and attempting to put it all right. She was a proud woman, and she was most proud of that stud farm of hers.

If there was a problem, she would wish to solve it herself.

Still. That didn't mean he had to sit here idle.

"Coulter, prepare a lad to take a note over to Godwin Place," Joseph said decidedly, rising to stand, his crutch carefully balanced.

His butler nodded. "Immediately, Your Grace."

By the time Joseph had reached his study, he had almost decided what to write. It did not need be a long note. Hattie understood him. She would know how desperate he was to see her.

Grabbing a pencil from the desk and not bothering with pen and ink, Joseph pulled a piece of paper toward him.

Hattie—

It feels like forever since I have seen you, and every passing minute makes it more unbearable. I love you, and I am sorry we missed each other yesterday. Come up to the house or stables whenever you want, they are open to you. It will all be yours in a few weeks anyway.

Please come tomorrow, at eleven o'clock. I have something rather interesting I would like to show you.

With all the love in the world from your future husband—
J. C. Wincham

Joseph glanced over the letter as he placed the pencil on the desk. Yes, it was perfect. Short, sweet. To the point. Emphasizing his affection for her and his need to see her.

Surely Hattie would have to reply to that, he thought as he carefully folded it and allowed a dribble of sealing wax to fall on the fold. He waited for just a moment, and then pressed his signet ring into the middle.

When he pulled his hand away, it was to see the curved W imprinted on the wax.

She'd open it immediately, his heart leaping as he handed the sealed note into the waiting hands of a stable lad. And he would see her tomorrow. Or perhaps even sooner! Perhaps she would not be able to contain her desire to see him and arrive tonight!

Joseph waited until midnight in the desperate hope her need for him would overwhelm her sense. The fire in the library died down slowly. He watched the embers curl. When he awoke the next morning, it was with a smile.

Hattie would be coming today.

There was no doubt in his mind as Joseph rose and dressed for riding. How would she stay away? It had been three whole days since they had seen each other. He ached for her as he had never known it was possible to ache for a person.

But she was his person. Joseph trotted down the stairs, crutch moving so fluidly now it was almost a second leg. His person that he needed.

So, where to greet her?

Eventually, he decided to seat himself on one of the chairs that lined the entrance way. All this walking and pacing over the last few days was playing havoc with his strength, and he wished to retain enough to go riding with Hattie later.

And so Joseph sat. And waited. And waited.

It was only when the grandfather clock chimed half past two o'clock that Joseph's heart skipped a beat.

Something was wrong.

It had to be. Hattie would not leave him like this—she would not agree to become his wife, allow him to make love to her, assure him she loved him and not his money, then disappear.

"—and then we should—Your Grace!"

Joseph looked up wearily to see his butler and a footman in discussion. The footman flushed and immediately disappeared into the servants' corridor. Was he the one Joseph had shouted at about the forks?

"I thought you would be on your ride with Miss Godwin?" Coulter said as he approached. "I did not expect you to be finished so soon."

Joseph swallowed. His mouth was unfathomably dry. "She never arrived."

"Never—never arrived?"

He stood up, suddenly filled with the absolute certainty he had to do something. He couldn't merely allow Hattie to fight all her own battles.

If they were going to be married—*when they were married*, Joseph corrected hastily—they would fight these things together. They would both put their best foot forward and stand side by side, against the odds.

Something was very wrong.

"I'm going out," said Joseph curtly as he strode to the front door.

"Out? Out? But where—Your Grace!"

Joseph paid him no heed. There was one purpose nestled in his heart now, and that was to ride over to Godwin Place and find out what had happened to Hattie.

His heart was beating frantically and there was a painful lurching in his stomach every time he took a step. Why had he waited this long? What if she was sick and had not called a doctor due to the expense? What if she was in pain?

"And send for Doctor Walsingham!" Joseph called over his shoulder.

"Doctor Walsingham? Are you unwell, Your—"

But Joseph was too far along the drive to hear his butler's pleas for explanations. The stables were in sight.

Some of the tension dissipated from Joseph's shoulders. There was something about horses, especially now. Maximus could have him at Godwin Place within the hour, then—

"Dear God," Joseph breathed as he stepped into his own stables. "What is going on?"

There were horses everywhere. Horses he did not recognize, large stallions which his men were struggling to contain. Mares that were skittish, one being gently approached by a stable lad who was whistling slowly.

Not his horses.

"Knowles!" barked Joseph.

In a moment, the stablehand had appeared by his shoulder. "Aye, Y'Grace?"

Joseph waited for the explanation which he presumed was clearly required. As the stablehand merely stared stonily, Joseph eventually exploded. "What the blazing hell—?"

And then his voice gave out.

A horse ran out between the stalls. A small horse, a tiny one. A foal.

Thunder.

"These are Miss Godwin's horses," said Knowles, rather unnecessarily.

Joseph's mouth was dry. What in God's name had happened up at that place—fire? But they had seen no smoke.

"What the—?"

"One of them was spotted out in the fields about an hour ago," Knowles said quietly in the mad rush of the stable. "I sent one of the men out with all the stable lads, and these were the horses they retrieved. I was about to send a message up to—"

But Joseph did not need to hear anymore.

He did not know what had happened up there at Godwin Place, but he didn't need to. Hattie loved those horses like they were children. She had pride in them far greater than most horse trainers. She would never have permitted them to ride out onto the fields, unchecked and without tack.

A devastating accident had happened.

"Maximus," he said curtly.

Knowles pointed to a stall. "It'll take me near on five minutes to saddle and—"

"We don't have five minutes. I'll ride bareback."

Only after the words had left his mouth did Joseph realize what he was saying.

Bareback? Him?

It had been simple enough in years gone by. He was one of the best horsemen in the area; there was nothing to be concerned about. Except…

Knowles's eyes were wide. "B-Bareback? You?"

Joseph's jaw tightened. "I may have lost a leg, man, but I will still happily lose your employ if you do not bring me Maximus this instant!"

It was perhaps an unkind thing to say, but he had more important things to worry about. Knowles surely knew he'd never lose his position at Cedarworth Lacey, but Hattie…

God knew what had happened to her.

Still, despite his bluster, Joseph was forced to realize he was about to undertake something he had never expected to do again. He had certainly not been trained for it. He and Hattie had never expected him to need to have to ride bareback. He would lose all the natural grip, the ability to direct the horse with a mere thought. But it would have to do. He couldn't wait.

With an ease he had never thought he'd have again, Joseph mounted Maximus and gripped part of his mane.

The stallion twisted his head, unaccustomed to the grip, but Joseph waited patiently.

He had ridden Maximus bareback several times. He would remember.

"You're best to take someone with you," said Knowles in a rush, following his master with a saddle in one hand and a pair of reins in the other. "I'll saddle up—"

"No, you go out looking for more horses," Joseph snapped. "Send Doctor Walsingham over to Godwin Place as soon as he arrives."

The stablehand's face went pale. "Miss Hattie—"

"I don't know," Joseph said wretchedly.

He hated how little he knew—he hated how long he had waited until he realized there was something wrong. If Hattie was unwell…if she died because of his inaction…

Knowles's face was resolute. "I'll find Miss Hattie's horses, Y'Grace, never fear. You tell her—"

Joseph did not wait to hear the rest. "Yah!"

His heel and stump kicked into Maximus's sides and the horse lurched forward, rushing into a gallop in an instant. Joseph held on for dear life, wondering if he would manage to reach Hattie in one piece.

What had she said about her competitors—those other horse trainers who would dearly love to have their hands on her horses?

Joseph's chest went cold. He had to rescue her. He had to show her he was willing to do anything to protect her, that he would never hold back when it came to saving her.

As long as he wasn't too late.

CHAPTER EIGHTEEN

December 29, 1810

HATTIE BLINKED BLEARILY. The light was too bright, but it had been since Edward had forced her into the kitchen. At least it was warm here…

"Hattie?"

Hattie moaned. She was waking up, and she didn't want to. When she was asleep, it was as if she had escaped from this nightmare.

Usually she had little time for sleep, preferring to spend as much of her time awake as possible. There was always so much to do. There were always her horses that needed her.

Her horses…

"How dare you come back here and steal from me!"

Tears threatened to fall as Hattie remembered the events of days ago. Two days ago? It was hard to tell. She had been kept here in the kitchen ever since.

Her horses—her precious horses. At least they had escaped rather than be taken by those odious men. Had one of them mentioned the Glasshand Gang? She could barely recall. So much had happened in the meantime.

"Hattie, you don't have to pretend to be asleep, you know,"

came Edward's dark voice with a chuckle. "I know you're awake."

Hattie swallowed and tried to prepare herself for another day with this brute.

She opened her eyes.

The kitchen was as it had been yesterday. The wide oak table had crumbs all over it—Edward was not a tidy eater—and he was still seated on a chair at the head.

She was seated on another chair, a little closer to the fire. Hattie supposed she was supposed to feel grateful. It was cold this December, after all. Somehow, she did not think Edward had thought about that.

"Good morning," said Edward cheerfully. "Are you going to play nicely today?"

And then despite her tiredness, despite the meager food Edward had given her, despite her fear, Hattie knew she would be resolute once more.

He could keep her here for a thousand years and she would not give in.

"No," Hattie said firmly.

Or at least, she would have done. She felt firm, but her throat was so dry it came out more as a croak than a statement.

The smile flickered on Edward's face then died away. "I beg your pardon?"

Hattie swallowed. "No."

How could she ever have imagined it would come to this? In all her years of knowing him, Hattie had never felt particularly warm toward Edward. She had told her mother countless times that she had a bad sense whenever she was around him.

But she could never have predicted this. Surely no one would.

Edward was shaking his head. "You know, I would have thought after a few days in my pleasant company, I may have been able to change your mind."

Hattie forced her tears back. She would not give him the satisfaction. "No."

"But we are engaged, Hattie! Engaged to be married!" Edward said as he leaned forward, a wild glint in his eye.

"We were never—"

"Your father thought it a most excellent suggestion," he said, cutting across her. "I believe he would have given his permission, had he lived long enough."

Though it was a terrible thought, for the first time in Hattie's life, she was glad her father had died when he had.

Mr. Godwin had been a good man. He had only done what he'd thought would be best for Hattie—and on paper, Edward was an excellent prospect. If only he weren't so abhorrent…

"I loaned you that money—"

"I paid that back," Hattie said sharply.

And greatly had she paid. Why the man thought he had some sort of ownership over her—she had paid him back, in full, with interest. And she had vowed to herself there and then.

She would never accept money from a man again unless she had earned it.

"Here I am, a horse trainer like you," said Edward, leaning back and spreading his arms wide. "I appreciate a horse, you know that. I even have a pretty good eye when it comes to breeding."

Hattie said nothing. The man was absolutely senseless. What did he think he was doing, keeping her captive in her own kitchen? Did he truly think he could wear her down?

When she had first realized what his intentions were, she had laughed. Keep her stuck inside, away from anyone else, until she agreed to marry him?

It was nonsense. He would see that, Hattie had thought when he had first dragged her in here, and release her.

But that had been…what, days ago?

Hattie stirred on the chair. "Can I walk about now?"

Edward glowered, but he had permitted her such things before. "Around the kitchen. Nothing funny, Miss Hattie, or I am afraid it will not go well with you."

She could well believe it. Though the man had not physically hurt her other than restraining her, Hattie was certain if pushed to it he would have no compunction in striking her.

And that would make it even more difficult to escape.

Wincing as she rose and stretched her legs, Hattie moved slowly around the kitchen in a circle. She made sure not to walk too close to Edward as she neared him, though it was difficult. Her kitchen was hardly large.

"You know, I knew I would marry you the first moment I saw you."

Hattie could not help but scoff. "You knew no such thing!"

"Oh, I did," said Edward firmly. His eyes were lit with a strange brightness. "I saw you across the village assembly. A country dance. You were dancing with your father."

Hattie did not recall. There had been many times that she had danced with her father. A woman who knew her own mind and was not afraid to share it was not often a welcome dance partner.

"And I knew then," Edward breathed, his gaze not leaving her as she circled the room. "I knew I would make you mine—"

"You cannot make anyone belong to someone," Hattie shot back.

That was a mistake. Her temper, though, had been restrained for too long. Ever since the fool had forced her inside and told her in no uncertain terms that she would not be allowed out until she agreed, again, to marry him.

"You promised yourself to me."

"I made a mistake!" Hattie said, heart breaking. "I took it back! It was long ago—"

"You think time can dull the feelings I have for you?" said Edward with a hurt expression. "You injure me."

Hattie swallowed as she walked slowly past the only window in the kitchen. It looked out on the stable yard. From here, she could not see any of her horses.

Which had escaped? Had any been stolen? Were those still in the barns and stables starving? Had anyone been there to care for them?

"You shouldn't be thinking of those damned beasts, you should be thinking of yourself!" snapped Edward.

Hattie glanced at him. He had evidently divined her thoughts. "You say you wish to marry me—"

"I *will* marry you," Edward spat, thunder in his brow. "You promised to marry me, Hattie, three years ago. You said you would, you gave your word!"

"And I retracted it the moment I realized what sort of a man you were!" Hattie shot back desperately.

He snorted. "You don't know what a good man is, you have no idea!"

She swallowed.

"I'm trying to tell you I'm in love with you, goddamnit!"

She would not think of him, Hattie told herself firmly as her heart fluttered. It was foolish to do so. Joseph was lost to her.

Oh, she would not marry Edward. She would rather rot here in her own kitchen. Besides, Betty would return from her parents' within a week. She would be found, eventually.

But the moment Joseph discovered she had been previously betrothed, that she'd kept that secret from him…

He'd been angry enough to discover she had kept her debts a secret. How much more angry would Joseph be when he found this out?

"But you think you do, don't you? You think you know love."

It was not a question, more a statement. Edward had spoken in such a strange, calm voice. He was smiling. Not a pleasant smile. This smile had a horrendous sort of pleasure in her misery.

"I don't know what you—"

"I think you do," interrupted Edward, pulling a piece of paper from his waistcoat. "Yes, I think you believe you know what love is because of a certain J. C."

Hattie's heart went cold. It wasn't possible—he was bluffing. He was giving the initials of a gentleman of the area, that was all. He could not possibly know—"

"'Hattie,'" Edward began reading from the paper. "'It feels like forever since I have seen you…'"

And that was when Hattie realized just how desperately she loved him.

Not Edward. Joseph.

He cared for her so deeply. The Joseph she had first met, the angry, embittered man who would not even accept her help in retrieving his crutch, could never have written those words. He may have felt them, but it would never occur to him to write them down.

But these words…he had only been without her three days. Yet he had felt compelled to write to her.

"Come up to the house or stables whenever you want, they are open to you. It will all be yours in a few weeks anyway."

"Why are you smiling?" Edward snapped, dropping the paper to the floor.

Hattie turned to face him, determined to speak. To tell him he could not cow her, he could not frighten her into acquiescing. Even if he did, after nights without sleep and days without food, he would have to drag her to a church and find a vicar willing to perform the ceremony against her will. Reverend McKee never would.

Because she would never marry him. She loved Joseph, loved him with all her heart.

And to be separated from him would be—

And she blinked.

It was because she was thinking of him, that was all. Her mind had been so lost in thoughts of Joseph that she was seeing a mirage of him, stepping slowly across the stable yard.

Hattie blinked. The image of Joseph remained.

He had come to rescue her.

"I said, why are you smiling?" Edward repeated. He rose from his chair, evidently furious. "I tell you, this letter is naught but desperation! This duke of yours will never marry you, not after he discovers you have been ruined by me!"

That got Hattie's attention. "But we never—"

"He won't know that," said Edward with a leer as he took a slow step toward her. "But you're right. I had better make sure, I suppose, that you are completely ruined in his eyes. And there's only one way to do that."

Hattie's heart went cold. Joseph had been walking toward the main house, not the kitchen. He wouldn't get to her in time.

Edward was advancing and there was nowhere to go. He had locked the door, the only key in his pocket. She would have to get near him to even have a chance of retrieving it, and if he grabbed her—

"Now then, Hattie, don't try to run," Edward breathed, his gaze flashing with malevolence. "It won't hurt, I assume—and there'll be no one to hear you scream."

It wasn't the threat he thought it was.

Of course, Hattie thought blindly. *Scream!* "Help!"

Her scream echoed around the kitchen, but she could not be sure how far it traveled. Had he heard her? Had Joseph realized she was being kept in the kitchen, not in the house?

Edward was laughing. "You see? There's no one to hear—"

"Hattie?"

Hattie's heart leapt. "I'm in here!"

She rushed to the kitchen door, hammering on it with both fists. He had to hear her! Joseph would soon realize where she was and—

But she wasn't swift enough. "Let me go!"

Edward's breath was warm and sticky on her neck, his hands grabbing her arms and pulling her back.

"Hattie?"

"I'm going to enjoy this," Edward moaned in her ear as Hattie struggled against him, calling Joseph's name.

"Joseph! Joseph, I'm—"

"Be quiet!" hissed Edward, clasping a hand over her mouth.

Hattie continued to try to pull free but it was no use. Edward was so much stronger than her, and Joseph had not arrived, and she was being pushed against the kitchen table—

The door burst open.

"Joseph," sobbed Hattie as Edward suddenly released her, turning in shock.

Joseph stood in the doorway, eyes blazing, rubbing his shoulder. He had evidently knocked the door down.

Which was impressive. Because Hattie couldn't see his crutch.

"This—*this* is the man you want over me?" Edward sneered, glancing between them. "Oh, you're well suited, I suppose. Hattie, the ruined woman, and Wincham, the ruined duke."

Rage, white-hot and unlike anything she had ever felt before, rushed through Hattie.

No one spoke to Joseph like that.

"How dare—"

But she was once again not fast enough. Though she had launched herself at Edward, unsure precisely what she was going to do but certain she wished him harm, Edward had taken a teasing step toward the duke.

"What are you going to do, run after me?" he guffawed.

And Hattie screamed, her hands flying to her mouth as Joseph punched Edward hard on the nose.

Edward went down slowly, crumpling into folds as he slid onto the floor. A trickle of blood oozed out of his nose. And then there was silence.

Silence, that was, other than Hattie's frantic breathing.

At first, all she could do was stare at the man who had become so obsessed with her that he had truly believed she would eventually go to him willingly.

As her senses caught up with her, Hattie's gaze lifted to the man she truly loved. The man who had come to rescue her.

"Joseph," she breathed.

Somehow, she was once again in his arms and Hattie almost wept with joy. This was where she belonged. This was the man she loved. This was the man who had risked much to come and rescue her, not knowing the danger, but evidently knowing something was wrong.

Oh, this man…

"Hattie, are you quite all right?" Joseph said, pushing her away to examine her, his gaze raking over her. "He did not injure you?"

Hattie swallowed. "I'm hungry, and tired—"

"I'll kill him," Joseph growled, bitter anger visible on his face. "He dared lay a hand on you…"

She hesitated. Hattie had no wish to protect Edward, but she was not sure if Joseph would seriously injure him. It would be a most unfortunate complication ahead of their wedding.

Still. She did not wish to lie. "He…he did not…there are no lasting—"

Joseph roared with unrestrained anger and tried to step toward the now senseless Edward.

But Hattie reached out to stop him. As he did not have his crutch, it was not difficult.

"No," she said firmly.

"But he tried to—"

"I know," said Hattie dryly. "Trust me, I know."

Joseph stared in amazement. "And you would let him live?"

"I would happily let him go to prison," she said with a laugh. "And his accomplices."

Joseph jerked around. "Accomplices? Where—"

"Oh, they left days ago," said Hattie, pushing back her hair and wondering if Joseph knew how to draw a hot bath. She was in dire need of one…

"Ah," said Joseph knowledgably, as though he knew the whole story. "They came for your horses."

Hattie blinked. Pain was starting to prickle at the corners of her awareness. It had been a long three days with only Edward for company, and he had hardly been concerned for her welfare.

"Horses?"

But the pain was not only physical. As she repeated the word,

Hattie thought of the horses she had lost thanks to the inept thieves.

Thunder. His mother. At least four other—

"Yes, I would imagine Knowles has them all by now," Joseph was saying, just out of earshot of Hattie's consciousness. "He has never failed me yet—"

"Wait—Mr. Knowles?" Hattie said, trying to take in what the man before her was saying. "What do you mean?"

"I mean, Knowles had Thunder and his mother in my stables this morning," Joseph said softly, lifting a hand to graze her cheek with his fingers. "And a stallion. I sent him out to look for others before I—"

"You did?" Hattie could hardly hold the tears back now. It had been such an ordeal, but she had not been the only living creature she had been concerned about.

Joseph nodded, smiling softly. "I know how much they meant to you—mean to you. I hope to return them to you in a few days—once Doctor Walsingham has seen to you, of course, and signed you off for riding."

There was so much new information circling in her mind, Hattie rather wondered that she could put any of it together.

"Doctor Walsingham?"

Joseph shrugged. "I sent for him before I left Cedarworth Lacey."

Which did not make sense, Hattie thought muzzily. "But how did you know—?"

"I didn't," Joseph said quietly. His gaze had never left hers, drinking her in as though she was the only water he had seen in days. "I just knew something had gone wrong. Something awful."

"How?"

"Well, I flattered myself that only that would keep you away from me for three days," Joseph said with a wry smile.

And Hattie did the only thing she could think to do. She pulled Joseph into her arms.

Their embrace lasted a few minutes. Or forever. Hattie

wasn't sure. All she could do was breathe in the rich masculine power of Joseph, feel the comforting strength of his arms, and know she would never have to be without him again.

When she pulled back, Hattie was blinking back tears. "You were magnificent, you know. I hope you see that."

Joseph laughed deprecatingly. "Oh, I'm not sure about that. I was terrified."

She stared up in wonder at the tall man. "Terrified?"

Now that was not an emotion she associated with Joseph, Duke of Wincham.

He nodded. "The thought that someone had hurt you…that you were waiting for me to realize something was wrong and it took me days to notice…oh, Hattie. I never would have forgiven myself."

Hattie's heart skipped a beat and affection rose in her chest. "You truly love me."

Joseph blinked. "Of course I do! You think I would come all this way with one foot for just anyone?"

She nudged him in the chest. "Joseph!"

"You know what I mean," he said with a laugh. "Now, are you going to kiss me?"

Hattie beamed as she returned to his embrace. "Yes. I'm going to kiss you now, and the next day, and the next day…"

Chapter Nineteen

January 7, 1811

"Joseph...Joseph..."

Every time Hattie breathed his name, Joseph could feel a flicker of excitement dart through his body. As though he only came alive in her presence. As though the longer they stayed together, the more he realized he had his whole life ahead of him.

A few months ago, he had thought his life was over. Joseph had been convinced that without both his legs, there was no point in living. What could he do other than suffer?

Now, as he stood in his stables, Hattie pressed up against an empty stall and his mouth trailing kisses down her neck, Joseph rather thought he'd found some very pleasant things to keep him occupied.

"Joseph," Hattie said firmly, her voice a little breathless. "We came here to ride."

Joseph grinned, mischief dancing in his eyes. "That is precisely what I have in mind."

"Joseph!"

But their laughter was unheard by anyone. Knowles had taken one look at Joseph as he'd marched across the stable yard, and ordered all the other servants into the kitchens.

"The master wishes to continue being trained by Miss Hattie," the stablehand had said with a wicked glint in his eye. "And I dare say he needs it."

If Knowles had not been so successful in retrieving all of Hattie's horses last week, Joseph might have had with a word with the impertinent man. As it was, he had far more important things to worry about.

Hattie's breath hitched in her throat. "No, really, we were going to ride!"

"And I told you," Joseph said, lips brushing against her collarbone, his gaze drifting to her décolletage. "We'll have a ride…"

His hands meandered to her hips and Hattie squirmed against him. Joseph swore under his breath. It was getting more and more difficult for the pair of them not to succumb to the pleasure they had already tasted.

After all, Joseph had attempted to argue only yesterday that they would be married in a matter of days. And, as Hattie had pointed out, he could wait until then.

That did not mean they could not enjoy themselves in other ways…

"The horses will need exercising," Hattie breathed, her head tilted back as she allowed him to continue kissing her.

Joseph shrugged, shifting on his foot to retain his balance. "And the fact you have not noticed there are no horses in my stable is, I think, a significant compliment to my lovemaking."

He should not have pointed it out.

Hattie stiffened, pulling away as her gaze darted about the stalls. "No horses—when were the horses taken away?"

She turned to him with an astounded expression that made Joseph chuckle. "The moment we came in here, Knowles removed the horses. I think he had a rather good idea of what I wished to do to you."

"But—but that means they all think we're," began Hattie, cheeks flaming. "Joseph!"

"Oh, let them think whatever they want," said Joseph with a

toss of his head. "What do we care?"

"Joseph, they are my neighbors!"

"In a few short days, they will be your servants," he pointed out, lifting his hand to cup her cheek. "Or have you forgotten?"

Hattie smiled as her cheeks continued to pink. "I am not accustomed to it, that's for certain."

It was going to be an adjustment for all of them.

Mrs. Alan, his housekeeper, had perhaps taken the news the best. "Oh, it will be wonderful to have a mistress in this place again! Please inform her, Your Grace, it is not my fault the curtains in the drawing room are in sore need of repair; it is Coulter who will not permit..."

The butler in question had been more sanguine. "I had expected as much."

And Joseph had raised an eyebrow. "You do not approve?"

"I approve of whatever you think is best, Your Grace," Coulter had said stoutly. And then his eyes twinkled. "Miss Godwin was always a good child, and I believe she has grown into a good woman. She may not have the breeding or the money, but she has the class."

That she did, Joseph thought as he tried not to immediately pull Hattie into the straw with him and pleasure her until she could stand no more.

Hattie Godwin was in a class far above him at any rate. For example, the fact she would soon be a duchess had been rather a shock to her system.

"You must have known that!" Joseph had laughed only that morning.

"But—but I can't be a duchess!" Hattie had stammered.

And he had smiled, and wondered how he had ever looked at her with disdain when they had first met. "You will be the most impressive duchess I have ever seen."

He was looking at her now with hedonistic eyes. Joseph groaned, attempting not to kiss her once again. It was proving more difficult with every passing hour. Every hour that brought them closer to their wedding.

"I can see the desire in your eyes," he murmured.

Hattie swallowed then wet her lips. "I—"

Joseph moaned. "Dear God, can't you see what you're doing to me?"

"I can feel it," Hattie said with a laugh.

Her hand slipped to his breeches and stroked his growing manhood.

"If you're not going to follow through on that, Hattie, I beg you—"

"I rather like the idea of you begging," she whispered.

And that was what did it. Try as he might, Joseph knew he would not be able to stand that sort of talk from a woman who looked that good in breeches.

He jumped a step back, holding his hands up. "I give up."

"You do?"

Perhaps it was Joseph's imagination, but Hattie looked disappointed.

"I did actually need to talk to you about something," Joseph said ruefully. "I had intended to bring it up in the house, but somehow I forgot about it until now."

Hattie raised an eyebrow as she stepped to the right and perched on a hay bale. "It must be important to distract you from riding me."

Joseph closed his eyes, just for a moment, to get his bearings. This woman was going to be the death of him—the worst of it all, there would be no better way to die.

"Joseph?"

"Just trying to collect myself," he said, opening his eyes to see Hattie's look of concern. "It's most strange. Something about you makes it almost impossible to think."

Her knowing smile caused a lurch of pleasure to roar through his chest. "I don't know what you mean."

She knew precisely what she meant. Joseph could see it in her eyes.

"This is serious," he warned, hopping over to another hay bale at right angle to hers.

As Joseph lowered himself onto it, his knee groaned with relief. He was still getting accustomed to standing for such lengths of time. His one remaining foot was not thanking him for it.

His stump grazed Hattie's knee as she looked worried. "Something serious? Edward?"

It was convenient that she looked away at that precise moment, or Joseph knew she would have seen the look of abject rage in his eyes. Thankfully, he was able to get his emotions under control when she turned back to him.

Well. Not completely under control. He still felt uncontrolled anger against the man who had attempted to force Hattie's hand—to demand it, in fact, in marriage.

How long she had waited there, in her own kitchen, a prisoner. How long she had wished for someone, him, to rescue her. And if he had not followed his instincts, how long would she have remained there?

Joseph swallowed. He'd had nightmares about it. Hattie, fading from lack of food or drink. Hattie, forced against her will. Hattie, dragged off to a church where a less than reputable vicar may have put aside all his morals for a little coin and married the two of them.

The fact Hattie was now safe, and well, and unharmed, did not negate how very in danger she had been.

"I am so sorry I did not tell you about him before," Hattie said in a rush. Her eyes were expressive. "I just, it was so long ago, and I had broken off the engagement the moment I realized—"

"I am not here to judge you for your mistakes," Joseph said quietly, placing a hand on her knee.

Hattie seemed to grow comfort from the connection. "I know. It's just—"

"He was the one in the wrong," he said firmly. "He was the

one who injured you, tried to rob you. He was the one who thought it acceptable to demand a woman's affections."

It was fortunate indeed his hand was on Hattie's knee. It prevented Joseph from curling it into a fist. *The blaggard!*

"And where…where is he now?" Hattie asked quietly.

Joseph sighed. "In prison, and likely to remain there. He gave up the names of his accomplices soon enough, and the involvement of the Glasshand Gang is no surprise."

"Remain there?"

"For years, I believe," Joseph nodded. "The magistrate dealt harshly with them."

Hattie raised an eyebrow. "I suppose it was unfortunate for Edward that you are the local magistrate."

He grinned. "Such a shame."

In truth, though Joseph would not own it to her or anyone, it had been difficult to remain impartial. Hattie may not be his wife, not yet, but he had considered her under his protection the moment they had kissed in that folly, giving of themselves in the only way they could.

After that, anyone who hurt Hattie hurt him. And though Joseph had been deeply injured before, the pain of losing his leg would have been nothing to losing the woman he loved.

"I am quite well, you know."

Joseph looked up.

Hattie was watching him closely, intelligence in her eyes. "I am not injured, not in body or in mind."

Joseph's voice was taut. "Anything could have happened to you. I should never—"

"There was no way you could have prevented this," Hattie said softly. "No one is to blame but them."

Joseph nodded, unable to speak.

His stomach lurched at the mere thought of what could have been. He pushed it away decidedly. There would be no nightmares, if he could help it. But he would never again be so debonair with Hattie's safety.

"Kiss me," he said aloud.

Hattie happily obliged. Joseph clung to her, relishing the sweet pleasure of her lips on his, the delicate way she tilted her head to allow him deeper. The eager way her tongue met his.

Oh, this was everything he wanted. Hattie, in his arms, safe and well.

When the kiss ended, they were both breathless.

That was surely why Joseph blurted out what he had really needed to talk to her about. "I have a decision to make."

Hattie raised an eyebrow. "Well, I would say Maximus is a tad old for breeding, but he does have an excellent line. I have a mare in mind, actually, which would—"

"Believe it or not, this is not about horses," Joseph said wryly.

His heart was pattering painfully in his chest. His heart rate had increased as they kissed, but it had remained high because he knew what he had to say.

And she might not like it.

"I'm going back to France."

Hattie started, eyes wide. "That's not a decision to make, that's a decision made!"

"The decision is not whether I will go to France," Joseph said hastily.

He knew he should have thought about this a little longer—but then, he had intended to wait to ask Hattie to marry him, and look what pleasures they had shared at their Christmas dinner when he had just leapt in, without a thought.

There was no more time to waste. He wanted everything out, open, for Hattie to know.

Secrets, after all, had only brought them pain.

"But—France?" Hattie looked worried, her eyebrows puckered into a frown. "How will you—your leg—"

"It is in an advisory capacity only," Joseph said quickly. "For some reason, they believe my strategy is worth having."

It had been a most surprising letter to receive. As it turned out, Chantmarle had mentioned again and again just how Joseph had made suggestions on troop movements, and with hindsight, he had been proven right.

Joseph had not even known the man had been recommending him for this position. It was most strange. But there it was.

"They need me there," Joseph said slowly. "And I need you."

He hardly had time to hold his breath before Hattie said, "I'll come with you."

Joseph blinked. Surely she had not—"It's a three-month posting, I will only be away from you for—"

"I said I will come with you."

Hattie was looking at him with such determination it took a moment for him to truly take in her words.

She could not be serious. France was no place for a lady!

His intention had been to ask her to move into his townhouse in London. She would be that much closer to the letters that way and he would not have to wait so long for a reply. That had been all.

All? It would be a great wrench for Hattie to leave her stud farm, Joseph knew. That had been the great favor he had been wishing to ask. That was the decision they would need to make together.

But this?

"I did not mean for you to come with me all the way to France," Joseph said swiftly. He took her hand in his and took a deep breath. "Having you in London would—"

"No, I'm coming to France," said Hattie sternly. "That is what I said, and you know I only say what I mean."

"You speak a great deal too much of your mind," said Joseph. "But you don't understand. I cannot risk having you—"

"You would be going," she pointed out. "You take the risk."

A bubble of frustration rose up and burst in Joseph's chest. Could she not understand? Could she not see just how awful his existence would be if he were to lose her?

It was bad enough that she could encounter such danger in her own home! What on earth would France present them?

"Hattie, when I was riding over to Godwin Place, thinking something awful had h-happened to you…" Joseph began. His voice had cracked. The agony in his soul could not be ignored. "My life would not be worth living, everything I am—"

"You think I could just wave you off to war without feeling the same?" Hattie interrupted fiercely. Her gaze blazed with determination. "Joseph, when you asked me to marry you, I was not ignorant of the vows we would take. For better, for worse. In sickness…and in health."

Despite himself, Joseph glanced down at his missing leg.

Strange. Sometimes, there were whole hours that he could forget it was not there. With his crutch, his walking now felt so natural it was hard to remember how things had been any different. When he was riding, he was just like any other man.

"For richer, for poorer," Joseph said with a laugh, meeting Hattie's eyes.

She had the good graces to look uncomfortable. "I've paid off all my debts, you know."

"I do indeed," he teased. "Though I would happily have paid them off for you, if you had told me about them."

Hattie grinned. "Why do you think I didn't tell you?"

Joseph returned her smile and wondered how he had ever managed to be so fortunate.

He was a duke, to be sure, but that did not offer a guarantee of happiness. It did not even offer a guarantee that one would keep all of one's limbs.

But as he sat here, in the quiet softness of his stables, the scent of straw and horses filling his lungs, Joseph knew he would never come close to this happiness without Hattie.

They…they appeared to be made for each other. He could not explain it.

Joseph's gaze raked over the beautiful curves and teasing smile of Hattie Godwin, and knew her internal beauty was far superior, though it did not seem possible. Her kindness, her boldness, the way she looked at him and spoke with derision if she thought he was being a fool…

There was no one like her. And though it would weigh heavily on his heart every day that they were in France, he would take her. If she insisted.

"I mean it," Hattie said softly, as though she could read his mind. "Wherever you go, I'll go. You put your best foot forward, and I'll be right alongside you."

"Even to France?" Joseph asked quietly. "Even leaving your horses, your stud farm?"

He held his breath as Hattie digested his words.

That, he knew, would be the biggest drawback to her suggestion. Going to France where there was a war going on? Oh, that was no trouble.

It was leaving Thunder and her other horses behind that was the problem.

"How long will we be in France?"

Joseph swallowed. "It's a three-month assignment. I am sure it would not be any longer."

He watched her consider, heart racing. He hardly knew if he wanted her to agree to come with him or not. But surely, if he was going to worry about her safety every day for the rest of his life, it would be better to have her with him? Where he could see that she was well?

Hattie took a deep breath. "I…I am going to entrust my stud farm to someone to care for it in that time."

Joseph blinked. "I beg your pardon?"

"Mr. Knowles seems to have a relatively good grasp of horses," she said airily, a flicker of that mischief he knew so well returning. "I suppose he cannot destroy the place completely in three months."

Joseph could not help but laugh. "Are you telling me you actually hold Knowles in relatively high regard? I thought you too were mortal enemies!"

"Joseph Chisholm!" Hattie said with a look of mock astonishment. "I have never heard anything so outrageous in all my life!"

"Well, in that case, here's something," Joseph said, leaning toward her. He could wait no longer. "I'm going to kiss you here in this stable, Miss Godwin—"

"Oh, are you?" she said, arching an eyebrow.

But Joseph saw with delight that she did not lean away. "And then I'm going to remove those breeches of yours—"

"Oh, are you?" Hattie said, her voice lower, her hands somehow pulling at the lapels of his coat, pulling him closer.

Joseph's manhood twitched. "I am indeed. And then I'm going to make you quiver all over with pleasure..."

Hattie whimpered, her eyelashes fluttering as he kissed her neck, his tongue teasing down her décolletage to her nipples. "Well, in that case, perhaps it's time I taught you a few things I've never taught anyone else..."

EPILOGUE

January 27, 1811

"AND YOU ARE absolutely sure?"

Hattie grinned as she spoke through the tent wall. "It's a little late for cold feet, don't you think?"

The wintery wind made the tent canvas snap and she shivered. It was far colder in France than she had expected. It was fortunate indeed she had secretly brought her breeches with her. None of the soldiers at the camp knew that underneath this gown, she was wearing them. Breeches did wonders for keeping the cold out.

"Cold feet?" came Joseph's voice through the tent wall. "Don't you mean cold foot?"

Hattie snorted with laughter. "Joseph!"

"What?" came his teasing voice. "If I can't jest about it, no one can!"

Hattie shook her head as she continued to laugh.

It was a miracle, really. The Joseph Chisholm, Duke of Wincham she had met on that cold November day would certainly never have considered even thinking about a jest over the fact he had lost a leg. But now Joseph could tease about it just as though it had barely happened to him.

It was another part of the healing, Doctor Walsingham had told Hattie before they left.

"But you don't think it's morbid?" she had asked anxiously, accosting the doctor before he left Cedarworth Lacey.

The doctor had shrugged. "It's a good sign, if you ask me. Anything that keeps a smile on a man's face is going to be approved of by this medical man."

"Are you sure, though?" Joseph persisted through the tent. "That you want a military wedding?"

Hattie looked around her. The small tent had been given to her by the company as a gift, to stay in before the wedding. The regiment, it appeared, could not countenance the thought of the Duke of Wincham and his bride-to-be already sharing a tent.

It was spacious enough for two, herself and her lady's maid. She had certainly bedded down in worse, like when Lightning had gone into a difficult labor with her foal. But she would be glad to be gone from it. She would be with Joseph.

"It's too late to cancel now," Hattie said through the tent. Really, it was most ridiculous that Joseph was attempting to keep to the old traditions! Why shouldn't he see her on their wedding morning? "I demand you make an honest woman of me!"

Joseph's snort was so loud she could easily hear it through the thick fabric. "You're altogether far too honest, Hattie Godwin."

"In that case, why aren't you at the altar?" Hattie said severely as her lady's maid Betty flittered about her, attempting to put her ear bobs in. "I'm ready!"

"My lady is not ready," Betty began.

Hattie waved her away. "I don't need adornments! Joseph knew what he was getting in for at Christmas."

Her cheeks flushed at the mere mention of that night. Oh, her whole life had changed that day…

"In that case, I'll see you there in five minutes," came Joseph's voice.

"I'll be there in ten," Hattie shot back. "You're the one who wants to keep all the traditions, and a bride is always late."

As it happened, she was genuinely late. Lifting her skirts above her ankles and striding happily through the mud, Hattie found herself turned around as she tried to find the tent which had been ordained, temporarily, as a church.

The trouble was, the camp all looked the same. Rows upon rows of identical tents, with soldiers in matching uniforms striding about the place. It was a wonder really that she managed to find her own tent every evening.

"That way, Miss Godwin," pointed a soldier with a flush. "Yonder."

Hattie saw a white flag flying over a tent slightly larger than the others. "Joseph," she breathed.

When the solider standing guard at the makeshift church saw her, he bowed then lifted up the tent flap.

Hattie gasped.

Though she had teased Joseph mercilessly the last week for his strict adherence to as many wedding traditions as possible, she had been sad not to have been wed in the village church.

It was where her parents had gotten married. She knew the aisle well, knew the nave. Had thought, one day…

So her mouth fell open as she saw Reverend McKee standing before a makeshift altar, just three pieces of wood nailed together, with Joseph beside him.

"Reverend McKee?" she breathed.

"And here I was, hoping that you'd be pleased to see me," Joseph quipped.

He was leaning heavily against his crutch—which only happened, Hattie knew, when he was nervous.

She knew how he felt. Marveling at the flowers that the troop had managed to find to adorn the tent, Hattie's legs trembled as she walked slowly up the middle. It wasn't quite an aisle. But it wasn't too far off.

"My dear Miss Godwin." Reverend McKee smiled. "You think I would have missed this? Your parents would have been so proud."

Hattie swallowed back tears.

She had not expected to feel so—well, overwhelmed. She was marrying Joseph and was absolutely certain she wanted to be his wife. She had thought the proceedings would be tedious until she could kiss Joseph and be happy.

But she was strangely moved to see such a familiar face. To know Joseph had organized such a thing to make her happy. He was going to be the most incredible husband.

"Hattie?"

Hattie blinked. Somehow, she was standing right beside Joseph, and at some point he had taken her hand, though she had not noticed when.

"Joseph," she breathed.

And everything made sense again. The world stopped spinning, her heart stopped thundering, and the tightness in her chest creeping up around her lungs dissipated.

Hattie beamed. "Ready to make an honest woman of me?"

The vicar coughed. "Dearly beloved…"

The wedding itself was precisely how Hattie would have wished it. Short. The only moment that seemed to elongate, stretching out, were their vows.

"…to have and to hold from this day forward, for better, for worse, for richer, for poorer, in sickness and in health, to love and to cherish…"

Hattie met Joseph's eye and saw the pain there, the hurt he had suffered. She saw the healing they had shared together, the love he felt for her, the acceptance of her path and his support of her future.

And she knew, without a shadow of a doubt, that being married to Joseph was the best step for her future happiness.

"—declare you man and wife!"

Joseph blinked. "Really?"

"No going back now," Hattie said cheerfully. "You're stuck with me. Forever."

"Well, in that case, I suppose I should start married life as I mean to carry on," said Joseph.

For a moment, she was not sure what he meant—then she gasped as he pulled her into his embrace and dipped her before bestowing a passionate kiss on her lips.

And the world faded away. There was no vicar, no officers standing and watching them. They were not in an English camp in a French field. There was no one else in the world.

Just Joseph and her.

When the kiss ended, Hattie's cheeks burned. "Joseph!"

"What, you thought I could resist?" he teased, righting her and looking red himself. "Come on—breakfast time!"

"Wedding breakfast time," Hattie corrected him with a laugh as she tucked her hand in his arm. "And I am absolutely starving. Where is it?"

It appeared Coulter, who had insisted to the point of tears on accompanying his master to his assignment in France, had placed quite a spread out on the table in Joseph's tent.

"My word!" said Hattie, her mouth falling open. "Coulter, you are a marvel!"

Hot buttered toast. Crumpets. Two kinds of eggs. What appeared to be kippers. Tomatoes, mushrooms, bacon—

"Only the best for the new Duchess of Wincham," the butler said, his cheeks rosy as he pulled out a chair.

Hattie swallowed as she took her seat opposite Joseph.

The new Duchess of Wincham.

It had been the one part of this she had tried to push from her mind. Being a duchess—having any sort of title, that was something that happened to other people. It didn't happen to little Hattie Godwin, daughter of Mr. Godwin who had frittered away his money by mismanaging his estate…

"Thank you, Coulter, that will be all," Joseph was saying smoothly to the butler.

The man bowed. "Just ring the bell if you need anything, Your Grace."

He left before Hattie could ask, "The bell?"

Joseph grinned as he pointed to something on the table between them.

Hattie's eyes widened as she saw the large silver bell with what appeared to be a mahogany handle. "He didn't bring the—"

"My butler is the best," Joseph said with a laugh, starting to pile food on his plate. "Our butler, I should say."

Warmth spread through Hattie's body. *Her butler. Her title. Her husband.*

It was all rather a lot to take in on one morning.

"I thought traditionally the wedding breakfast was in the afternoon," she pointed out as Joseph poured her a cup of tea. "With one's friends and relations."

"Well, I have no relations, and most of my friends are either in London or meandering about the French countryside," said Joseph with a teasing air. "You know, I never thought I'd be back here. It's most strange."

Hattie knew better than to jump in with her opinion. That was one of the things she was fast learning about her new husband. He often spoke aloud to untangle his own thoughts, and if someone else jumped in, he was liable to lose his train of thought.

"After losing my leg, well, I had rather hoped I'd seen the back of this place," Joseph said ruefully.

Hattie waited then prompted, "I suppose your military strategy and my knowledge of horses makes us valuable here. Important."

Joseph snorted. "Something like that. Though I would argue it's people like—well, Chantmarle and some duke I've never heard of, Fitzpaine, they're the ones who could make the real difference in this war. With them on our side, somewhere in France I believe, we should do well."

Her stomach lurched.

It had been quite an adjustment, coming to France. She had read about the country, learned its history, read its literature. She had even learned enough of the language to passably converse, at least she thought so.

But it was altogether quite different, being here.

"Fitzpaine?" she repeated. "I have never heard of that particular duchy."

Joseph shrugged. "I have never heard of him either, which is why my circle is agog with news about him. A most curious fellow, he appeared just when we needed him, too. He may be the key to ending this nonsense. If we can get a hold of him, of course. Terribly hard to pin down, this Fitzpaine."

"You think the war could be over soon?" Hattie asked softly.

Joseph's hand, holding a fork that was piled high with bacon and eggs, halted. "No," he said quietly, meeting her gaze. "We could be here for some time."

Hattie nodded sagely as Joseph shoved the food hungrily in his mouth. "Well, not longer than the three months agreed, surely?"

They had already been here two weeks. Just another ten, she told herself, and they would be back on their way home. A new home, together.

Joseph shrugged. "There's already talk of staying a few months longer."

Hattie's smile faltered. "Truly?"

"Maybe upward of five months—oh, in total, not an additional five months," he added swiftly, seeing her face. "Eat up, you haven't touched your breakfast. I want you in fine fettle; you're going to need your strength for later."

His teasing smile told Hattie in no uncertain terms precisely why he wished her to be strong. They had been tempted, yet not succumbed while in France. She sorely missed him.

But as her stomach lurched at the thought of eating this early in the morning, Hattie merely raised her teacup to her lips and sipped the pleasantly hot water.

No, this was not the right time. Joseph had been through so much and he was already so worried about her. The last thing he needed was another reason to worry—

"Perhaps even seven months," Joseph continued, happily eating his hot breakfast. "I've told the captain here, if we're here a year he'll owe us a guinea!"

Hattie's stomach swooped. "Well, in several months we will have to return to England, whether or not the war needs you."

Joseph had been about to drink some of his own tea, but he placed the cup on the saucer with a surprised expression. "Why?"

A slow smile started to creep over Hattie's lips. *Well, why not?* They were unlikely to be alone, truly alone, for some time. And he needed to know. He would soon guess, she was certain, once Betty moved her things into his tent.

"Because," Hattie said gently, not taking her gaze from his. "Because I believe the heir to the Wincham title should probably be born in England."

Joseph stared. The words, it appeared, would not sink in.

Hattie cleared her throat but said nothing. He needed time…

"Heir," he repeated, eyes widening as comprehension began to dawn. "Heir to—to the Wincham title?"

Hattie nodded, joy bursting within her. "I would not wish to—I spoke to Doctor Walsingham just before we left, and he seemed certain—"

"Hattie you're not—you're not with child, are you?" Joseph breathed.

She nodded again.

Joseph swiftly rose from his seat, crutch forgotten, as he knelt on the wooden floor built for their comfort when the Duke of Wincham had arrived at the champ. He hobbled forward on his knees, eyes never leaving Hattie.

"Oh, Hattie," Joseph breathed, taking her hands in his and kissing the tips of her fingers. "I don't think there's anything you could have given me better than this."

Joy spread through her chest as Hattie looked at the man who had given so much.

Not a title. Not money—she had been very clear about that before they had left for France. No, he had given her his love, and that was better than any plans she could have made for herself.

Then Joseph's face clouded. "But—but a baby? Here? Hattie you should never have come. What are we going to—"

Hattie stopped his concerns with a kiss. He melted into her, and when she broke the kiss, there was a look of contentment across Joseph's brow.

"Well, wherever you take me, you wild woman," Joseph said wryly, "as long as I have you, I can put my best foot forward."

And as he lifted his lips up to be kissed once more, Hattie was certain: every step would be perfect, as long as they were together.

About Emily E K Murdoch

If you love falling in love, then you've come to the right place.

I am a historian and writer and have a varied career to date: from examining medieval manuscripts to designing museum exhibitions, to working as a researcher for the BBC to working for the National Trust.

My books range from England 1050 to Texas 1848, and I can't wait for you to fall in love with my heroes and heroines!

Follow me on twitter and instagram @emilyekmurdoch, find me on facebook at facebook.com/theemilyekmurdoch, and read my blog at www.emilyekmurdoch.com.

www.ingramcontent.com/pod-product-compliance
Lightning Source LLC
Chambersburg PA
CBHW070345200726
48294CB00003B/791

9781961275539